DEATH IN THE MIRROR

A Poison Ink Mystery

BETH BYERS

SUMMARY

September 1937

Georgette Dorothy Aaron is expecting a bundle of joy, focusing on updating her house, writing books, and enjoying her family. What she's not doing is meddling. She's not sticking her nose in other people's business. She's not writing books about her neighbors. She's determined to turn over a new leaf and slide right back into the safety of being a wallflower.

Georgette, however, gets stuck on her book, sick of the smell of drying paint, and decides to take a ramble. When she stops to check herself in the mirror, she doesn't expect to see someone else in the reflection. Nor does she expect what happens next.

❧ I ❧

I f one were to glance at the village of Harper's Hollow from on high, the first thing noticeable would be the curving quiet river rolling through the center of the town. It was, simply put, idyllic. Bicyclists rode along the paths next to the river. Others walked their dogs, or children ran escaping into the afternoon sunlight. If one walked long enough, the next show-stopper was the brick and stone bridge that arched over the water with tunnels beneath to provide passage for the boats. To float beneath that bridge was pure romance.

The church was in a fabulous square, but it wasn't one of the great cathedrals. It was respectable to say the least, however, and perhaps just short from comparison to one of the more notable places of worship by its age and the obvious care taken in its construction. Beyond, the square where the church stood, one could wander down the cobblestone streets and enjoy the sheer beauty of the village.

A hungry soul could stop in at the pub, where an excellent brew could be accompanied by quite fabulous fish and chips, or dive into a memorable bowl of chowder. If the visitor were of a more adventurous nature, they might well ramble through the hedges, the trees, or the fields of green. They weren't going to find the gothic romance of the moors but could find a place for quite an excellent picnic in nearly every vista.

For Georgette Dorothy Aaron, however, the shine on the village had disappeared. She had, after all, found a body in the attic of her dream home and been embroiled in—yet another—murder investigation. She was starting to wonder if there was something about her that attracted the terrible events. Perhaps Harper's Hollow wasn't what it could have been, but she was practical enough that she did not regret her move. Georgette had, after all, written a book based off her neighbors that had resulted in not one, or even two, but several murders.

She had well and truly fled the neighbors and friends of her childhood and wanted nothing more than to disappear back into obscurity in her new village. She was not, however, the same creature as she had once been. It seemed that when one transitioned from old maid to married woman, from poor soul to better-off author, from childless to the guardian of three orphans, it was much more difficult to fade into the background.

The reality of Georgette's new life was one that the goddess Atë enjoyed very much. Atë, goddess of mischief, had turned her impish and uncomfortable eye on poor Georgette, and Atë's ruinous curiosity abounded. If Georgette was placed in a position where she had to speak in public, would she sound like another boring housewife?

Or would that wicked sense of humor and honor reveal itself? The same mind that illustrated her neighbors' lives and gave them the endings that seemed appropriate— what would it do in a village meeting?

Atë's devilish gaze leapt from target to target as she debated wayward souls, dirty tricks, and transgressions. What if...Atë smiled and considered. She wanted to see shenanigans in the offing. Hijinks were acceptable.

What was not acceptable? A staid afternoon writing wholesome fiction about a sweet little town and the ethical inhabitants wouldn't do at all. Neither would an afternoon of planning out the next stage of the nursery. A light debate about names for her coming child? No. An excess of tea? Absolutely not. Surely there was something. Atë didn't need a catastrophe, but she'd happily accept a bit of sportive roguery.

GEORGETTE DOROTHY AARON

"Darling Georgie," Charles said as he straightened his coat and shuffled through the contents of his briefcase. "Do you truly think that you're feeling all right?"

"I'm quite all right, Charles."

"You're green, darling."

"That is the paint in the nursery drying. It would leave anyone a bit headachy." Especially when scents were so harsh since she'd realized she was expecting and it seemed every little smell paraded through her nose.

Charles had engaged in the habit of turning her to face him during the course of their courtship, and it was a comforting one now. He pressed a gentle finger under her chin, turned her face up to him, and left a gentle kiss on her forehead, followed by a more fervent one on her lips. She smiled against his mouth and felt his corresponding grin. His hand trailed down her back and slid around to feel their baby, which revealed itself with nothing more than a slight bulge of her waist.

"Are you sure you are quite all right, darling?" The worry in his voice was warming, Georgette had to admit. There was something about being in someone's loving thoughts that made her a touch emotional. That could, of course, be the babe she was growing—she'd become a weeping willow in addition to smelling every possible scent, sicking up far too often, and generally being exhausted. Every aspect of her life was being affected by the child, and he or she wasn't even here yet.

"Of course I am," she said, fighting any sign of tears. It would leave dear Charles worried all day if he left her weeping. "All I need is tea, toast, and perhaps a bit of a ramble."

"You'll take the dogs?"

Georgette was quite kind, especially to those she loved, so she did not roll her eyes at him, huff, or sigh heavily. Instead she pushed up on her toes and kissed the bottom of his chin. "Certainly."

"Perhaps Lucy?"

"Charles—" Georgette wasn't a saint, so there was the hint of an edge to her voice. "I will be careful, I will walk until I feel better and not until I am exhausted, I will take the dogs, and I will be sure to tell Eunice where I am going. Perhaps I will even convince her to abandon her post and ramble alongside. Lucy will, of course, be invited."

"Excellent idea," Charles said with an unrepentant grin. "When does Marian arrive?"

They eyed each other with a careful, silent debate. They had been told a few too many times that they were "set in their ways" and "likely to butt heads" due to the years of solitary living. Perhaps they would have, if they weren't more determined to prove their naysayers wrong. As though an eighteen-year-old couple were somehow likelier to find happiness simply because they hadn't learned their own minds yet.

Georgette and Charles benefitted from the wisdom of age. After all, newlyweds or not, they were not bright young things. They'd grown alone, lived alone, made their way through life alone, and when they'd found each other, it was rather like finding someone you had loved and not remembered.

Georgette had longed for love. It was as if someone who should have been there was missing from her life, and she missed them. All the same, she had little faith that someone ever would even notice her, let alone love her. Charles, on the other hand, had opportunities for love but no one had seemed worth the trouble. Until Georgette that is. It was when she appeared in his life that he realized the hole in it that only one person could complete.

"Georgette darling," he said carefully, wanting to leave her happy, "it's only because I adore you and love you that I worry."

"Charles darling," she said with a rare wicked grin, "it's only because I adore you and love you that I have yet to box your ears."

His laughter sang out to her, and he took her face

between his hands, leaving a gentle kiss on each eyebrow, the tip of her nose, and her lips before offering his arm to lead her down to the dining room.

Georgette's stomach had little appreciation for anything but tea, and Charles cared more about her than he did about his usual breakfast of bacon and poached eggs. Their sideboard was a touch naked these days. Breakfast buns, fruit, and bread next to the toaster. Georgette ignored it all for the orange and cinnamon tea that she made with an excess of milk and sugar. It was possible to live on tea, wasn't it? This baby had decided to help Georgette discover if it was true.

Charles made himself a stack of toast to counteract the lack of eggs and bacon, and they ate in silence while he read the newspaper. The quiet of the home after the weeks with children had become too stark, Georgette thought. Charles had decided a few weeks after they'd taken the three orphaned siblings in that if they were going to see them raised, they would raise them in the same manner as they would raise their own children.

Georgette fully endorsed the idea. She hadn't wanted to broach it after having brought them home without even asking his opinion. Once the decision had been made, Eddie was sent to study with a tutor in the lake country. He'd finished school the year before at 16-years-old and was ready to go to the university. If he wanted to go to the university, he needed to prepare. At twelve, Janey had been sent to school where she could come home on the weekends, and at nearly-eighteen, Lucy remained with them. She was an inexplicably early riser who got up with the birds, ate with Eunice, and spent her days trying to decide what she wanted to do now that she was finished with school.

Georgette opened the window to her bedroom after Charles left and returned to bed. There was something so luxurious about going back to bed after eating, and Georgette felt as though her headache justified the choice.

She stayed in bed until the nausea passed and her headache was less intense. There was a dog on each side of her when she shifted, and Georgette rubbed her face with each of them before she hauled herself out of bed and down to the garden. Eunice had already left, Lucy was drawing in the front parlor, and Georgette thought that a few minutes alone walking and thinking about her book options was the better course of action.

It seemed when she first wrote The Chronicles of Harper's Bend that the idea of writing a book was impossible. She had no imagination, she told herself, so she wrote about her neighbors, gradually transitioning to full fiction.

Her next, fully fictional novel, Josephine, had appeared in her mind as though it wanted to be told. The idea had presented itself, grew in the quiet moments, and abounded about Georgette's head until she'd written it to free herself from the knocking at the door of her mind.

Now, however, she had finished another Harper's Bend book but wasn't sure where else to go. Josephine's story had been told and the character had stepped out of Georgette's mind as abruptly as she'd entered.

It was Lucy, Eddie, Janie, and the baby on Georgette's mind as she walked. Education, nannies, wardrobes. Georgette fiddled with her wedding ring as she walked. She'd had success with her first attempts at writing. Could she do it again? Did she dare try something different? If she did, would she lose those readers who had already found and enjoyed her writing?

There was a part of her that wondered if she should focus on the art of writing, but Georgette knew that she'd started writing in the attempt to keep herself from becoming homeless or slowly starving and surely there was a way to combine writing with supporting their family?

❧ 2 ☙

GEORGETTE DOROTHY AARON

The trio of dogs ranged ahead of Georgette as she made her way through the woods. The birds were singing, the wind was snapping through the branches, and the scent of fresh air was cleansing after the drying paint. It had rained early that morning and the clean fresh scent was so delightful that Georgette took repeated deep breaths, pausing to enjoy it.

Georgette considered her route and then veered towards the deeper wood. Once she ranged through the trees and down the path, the wood poured out into quite a lovely orchard with apples that were ripening. The owner of the orchard was happy enough to let those who wandered in pick a few. Katherine Lynd was a widow, a lover of tea and books, and one of Georgette's favorite people in Harper's Hollow. It was a bit of a ramble to reach her, but her conversation was well worth the lengthy walk.

Katherine wasn't in the orchard, and the outer garden was empty, and there was no answer at the door. Georgette followed the long path away from the house and towards the road, planning to circle back to her own house, when the wind picked up. She was showered with rainwater from the tree boughs and she gasped. The top half of her dress was covered in a spatter of rain and a few fallen leaves, and she was instantly chilled despite the sun.

Georgette took a long breath in as she picked off the few leaves clinging to her before she pulled forward her leather bag and took out her handkerchief. She wiped her face then pulled out the sweater she'd brought only because she'd heard Charles's worried voice in her head about the chilly weather. Another leaf dislodged from her hair as she pulled on the sweater.

Georgette walked forward and leaned against the stone fence that surrounded Katherine's property before digging through her bag. The compact that Marian had insisted she carry was there. Feeling self-conscious, Georgette opened it to examine her hair and plucked out another leaf. She realized she could see a small area behind her when she angled the compact just so. A little and entirely unwanted part of her wondered how easy it would be to spy on someone in such a way.

She was debating the warmth of her sweater against returning home or carrying on more briskly when there was a loud crack. Georgette gasped and her dogs burst into barking. She placed her hand against her chest and breathed in deeply, trying to regain a measure of calm.

Susan's head tilted at Georgette and she laughed at her

dog, reaching down and scratching the dog's ears while she licked Georgette's hand frantically. Georgette opened her compact again, noted the sudden flush to her skin, but she was distracted by the burst of birds above the trees behind her.

One of the dogs whined and Georgette glanced down, not entirely sure which it was when Susan barked and darted towards the trees where the birds were circling. Georgette started to call her dog when she was struck by a chilling thought.

What if?

No, she thought. The dog running towards that part of the wood meant nothing. And the noise could have been anything, such as an automobile backfiring.

But still—Georgette scrunched her nose, knowing her imagination would run wild until she had verified that the dog's mark was nothing more than a rabbit. Georgette sighed and followed Susan. The closer they got, the more the dogs vocalized their distress.

Georgette placed her hand on her chest as she scooped up Dorcas with one arm. The dog whined and wriggled as if trying to get closer to Georgette when she heard a low moan. It wasn't one of her dogs, but Susan went wild in barking as Georgette rushed forward. She let go of Dorcas as she dropped to her knees by a prone woman, who moaned again as the dogs circled them.

"Katherine?"

Georgette took the woman by the shoulder and turned her slowly, surprised to see a woman with light brown hair, light blue eyes, and a round face. It wasn't Katherine, who was older. The woman moaned again and

Georgette looked towards Katherine's house. Her friend didn't have a phone.

"Stay!" Georgette said to her dogs and then ran towards her house. She wasn't a runner and her lungs clenched, but she didn't let herself stop. She considered her options and decided she would risk going for the Mustly's house instead of her own. If Barnaby Mustly was home, he could help her with the woman while his wife summoned more help.

She held her side as she nearly collapsed against their door. She had run several kilometers when she normally wandered sedately, especially since she'd gotten with child.

Anna opened the door and Georgette stumbled towards the woman. "I'm sorry, Anna," Georgette huffed. "There's a hurt woman by Katherine's."

"A woman? Barnaby!"

Georgette held her chest again. "Oh my goodness, I need to exercise more."

"A woman?"

Georgette nodded. "There was a sound. It was loud and then birds."

"Birds?" Barnaby asked kindly.

"Birds and then Susan barked, and I thought if I don't check, I'll wonder and think about it, and at 2:00 a.m., I'll end up dragging Charles to check, so I went to look."

"Where is the woman, Georgette?" Barnaby asked patiently. Georgette realized that in her distress and exhaustion, she was babbling.

"By Katherine's. I'll show you."

She rose weakly as Barnaby nodded. "The auto is out

front. Anna darling, call the police station and for the doctor."

Once they were in the auto, Barnaby motored towards Katherine's house.

"We have a new doctor?" Georgette asked.

"We do." He smiled at her. "What happened?"

Georgette considered and then shook her head. She really had no idea at all. "She was just there. She was on her face. I turned her over. Maybe it was a sort of...of... internal attack? I was so afraid it was Katherine that I have to admit I was relieved it wasn't her and then I was relieved that the woman was alive."

Georgette's hands were shaking, but she'd caught her breath. Barnaby noted the shift in her and said, "You know, Charles is going to lose his mind that you went running through the wood after finding a poor woman hurt and alone."

She laughed, but it wasn't all that funny really. The last thing she wanted to do was stress her poor husband. "I'm sure it was only an accident."

Georgette thought back. The noise, the birds, the poor woman. She rubbed her forehead and then glanced towards Barnaby. He was frowning as well.

"The wind had picked up," Georgette said, knowing she was struggling towards an answer for what had happened to the woman. "Then there was the noise, like a crack. The noise couldn't be part of it if the problem was inside her."

"She might have fallen or tripped?"

Georgette pictured the woman and then shook her head. "No, I'm quite sure she was lying in a clear space. I'd have noticed a collapsed chair or bench. Even a large rock. Or a tree limb," she added, recalling her earlier thought of a fallen limb.

"A coincidence, then," Barnaby declared.

"Unless it isn't." Georgette winced at the thought. "And the noise is part of it."

"You think it could have been an attack?"

Georgette shook her head, uncertain or unwilling to consider it.

"If it was an attack," Barnaby said, "who would do that to a stranger near Katherine's?"

"Maybe they intended to hurt Katherine?"

The two exchanged looks and then shook their heads in unison. Katherine was a widowed grandmother who made pies for the neighborhood, biscuits for children who stopped by, who had the most beautiful hobbyist flower garden that Georgette had ever seen. There was no reason for anyone to harm the woman.

"We're jumping to conclusions because of our history," Barnaby suggested. "Dr. Fowler makes us seen villainy where there is nothing."

"It is odd, though, isn't it?"

Barnaby brought the auto to a halt and they both rushed out and towards Georgette's dogs. She heard one of them howling and was sure that it was poor Dorcas. The gentlest and most nervous of her dogs darted towards Georgette the moment she hurried into the clearing. Georgette scooped her up, comforting her through the low whine as Barnaby dropped down next to the woman.

"She's breathing," he said, "but she's not waking."

"I heard her moan," Georgette said, kneeling next to him. Georgette took the woman's hand, tucking her dog,

Dorcas, next to her side while she felt for a pulse. "She's alive."

Barnaby stood and hurried to the auto, returning with a blanket that he laid over the woman. By the time they'd tucked the blanket around her, an ambulance arrived along with the constable and the new village doctor.

"Georgette," Barnaby said as they stood away with the dogs while the doctor hunched over the body of the woman. "Look."

She turned and her breath caught. Under the ferns of the nearby tree was a large wooden shape. It was too straight to be a tree branch, but the right shape to be a fence post. She met Barnaby's gaze, who met hers in return. They mirrored each other's horrified expressions. Slowly, the two of them approached the wooden object with Barnaby slightly in the lead with the dogs hanging back, but Georgette had her hand on Barnaby's arm as if she needed to be able to yank him back.

The broken fence post had been tossed recently onto the ferns, bending back several fronds. The sharp corner of it was smeared with red that couldn't possibly be paint.

"Georgette—" Barnaby said with caution in his voice. It matched the growing concern in her. "I think...I don't think that...I—"

"I don't think this was an accident," Georgette finished. They grasped each other's wrists tightly and then both looked back. A young man was helping the constable lift the woman onto the stretcher. Georgette hadn't noticed in her distress that the woman was a larger round woman. The two men struggled to get her into the back of the auto.

"Why would anyone hurt this woman?" Barnaby muttered.

Georgette shook her head, shivering. She'd been so close to the event. What if she hadn't hesitated to look for the reason of the noise and the flying birds? What if she'd wandered into the attacker? What would have happened to her and her baby? She shivered as she placed her hand over her stomach.

"Do you know her?" she asked Barnaby.

Barnaby shook his head and then paused. He frowned as he turned. "You know—I might."

"Who do you think she is?" Georgette asked as the constable approached.

Higgins was a good man, prepared to deal with the occasional family squabble, lost dog, stolen bicycle, or whatnot. What he was not prepared to deal with, however, was a murder, a malicious attack, or the same.

He had overheard Georgette's question to Barnaby and repeated it after a solemn greeting to them and the dogs.

Barnaby answered. "I think she might be one of Katherine Lynd's daughters-in-law. The one married to John Lynd."

"I didn't know Katherine's family was visiting," the constable said. In a village as small as Harper's Hollow, visitors were quickly noticed.

Barnaby shook his head. Both of them had seen Katherine in the last few days, Georgette was sure. Surely, she'd have said if she expected any of her children to come. Maybe they came unexpectedly? No, Georgette frowned. Usually Katherine went to visit them. Something about managing children on the train.

"Where is Katherine?" Georgette asked.

No one could answer.

They searched for her together. Barnaby refused to split up when Georgette suggested it, muttering about Charles, safety, and fiends attacking women in the daytime. The dogs helped as best they could, sniffing around bushes and trees. They had only just finished searching Katherine's property when Charles and Joseph arrived. The constable must have telephoned them, no doubt because Anna had mentioned Georgette's name when she called to report the injured woman.

Uncle and nephew stood side-by-side as Georgette and Barnaby exited the orchard. Hands on hips, faces hidden by the shadows since the sun was behind them, they would have made a striking pair if not for the dogs darting around their legs, having raced ahead to greet them.

"Poor Charles," Barnaby said. "How many bodies are you going to trip over?"

Georgette bit down on her bottom lip to keep from answering. How many? Barnaby had no idea of the events that linked to her writing and the murders that had occurred. He only knew of the girl who'd been killed long before Georgette and Charles had moved into the village. What would her friend think if he knew the whole of Georgette's history and the bodies she'd stumbled over? At least this one wasn't dead.

❧ 3 ❧

GEORGETTE DOROTHY AARON

Anna Mustly appeared in the wood about the same time that Charles dropped his hands from his hips and crossed to Georgette. He took her hand, squeezing tightly, and then tugged her close.

"Are you all right?"

She nodded against his chest.

"You're a bit pale."

"It's been a bit startling," she told him, glancing beyond her husband to his detective and nephew. "Joseph, how are you?"

He grinned at her and when Charles looked away, winked. "What's all this? You were drawn to the scene of what we think is a crime by a—what? Mischievous spirit?"

Georgette's expression was long-suffering. The sound of his voice told her he wasn't all that worried. A blustery day, a branch on the back of the head. He didn't think what she and Barnaby thought, and he'd moved straight to teasing her. "I was escaping paint fumes."

"No one smells those but you," Joseph told her with enough of a smile to tease her.

"No one but me is expecting a bundle of joy." She glanced at Charles with a silent order to make Joseph leave her alone. She hadn't realized that taking on Charles's nephews as family meant having little brothers, even though they'd all met as adults. "I'll be sure to torment Marian when it's her."

His happiness faded and Georgette winced. Their wedding plans had not been going well lately.

"I'm not sure what being an expectant mother has to do with it, darling Georgie," Joseph finally said. "It's that over-active imagination of yours." He peered beyond her. Katherine Lynd's daughter-in-law had been taken away and the constable had stayed long enough to be sure that there wasn't anyone about. Georgette's and Barnaby's search for Katherine, in case she was hurt too, had turned up nothing. They hadn't found her, but they'd be more at ease knowing they'd looked.

"Do you really think it wasn't an accident?" Joseph asked.

"The wind did pick up, but she wasn't hit by a falling branch. She was hit by a fence post."

Joseph looked up in surprise by that. The idea that Georgette had been a bit too imaginative changed and instead the cloak of a police officer came over him. "A fence post?"

"I believe so," Georgette answered, glancing at Barnaby who nodded. "We've been quite worried about Katherine, but she doesn't seem to be about."

"Of course she isn't," Anna cut in. "She volunteers at that orphanage near Ely on Thursdays." Anna gave Barnaby a disbelieving look that he hadn't remembered.

"Does she?" Georgette asked, feeling an instant rush of relief. She hadn't realized quite how worried she'd grown. Katherine was the woman who made cookies for the village's children to come by, the woman who brought flowers to every home with a sick woman, the woman who was the first to volunteer. The idea that anything could have happened to her, it was more than Georgette was prepared for, especially with her heightened emotions.

"Thank goodness," Barnaby said, sounding as relieved as Georgette. "I'm not prepared to lose another one of us. I just—" He shook his head and glanced away. He'd been close to the girl who had died and been left in Georgette's attic, mourning almost as much as her family. "I can't do it again."

"I'm going to look around," Joseph told them. "Take these ladies home, gents. I'll be by to see what there is to know later."

Georgette let Charles lead her to the auto and when they were both seated with the dogs in the back seat, he paused long enough for her to look up and examine him.

"Georgette," he said quietly. "Tell me you were careful."

"I was careful," she replied.

"Tell me you weren't in danger."

She paused at that and then said, "I believe the dogs would have let out quite a ruckus if I had been, and Charles, I would never put our baby at risk. I only went for a walk and thought I'd check in on Katherine."

He took her hand and lifted it to his mouth before reversing the auto and backing onto the street. The drive was mere minutes, but with his thumb moving over the back of her hand, it seemed forever.

"Did you know there was a new doctor?"

He shook his head. "I'd rather we stick with the fellow we found."

Georgette smiled. "I'd never disregard all the work that Robert put into finding the fellow for us." Charles's other nephew, Robert, had helped not only in locating a good doctor, but also the village itself. "Did you know? There's a rather nice set of rooms near the train station here. Something appropriate for a bachelor like Robert."

Charles laughed. "I think that our bachelor prefers his life a bit livelier than Harper's Hollow. There's no chance he'll even consider a move, darling, until one of you ladies traps him with a love of his own. Then, he'll be ready to settle here."

"Maybe her family will want her closer." Georgette's mouth screwed up at the thought and she muttered, "We need to get him before he meets the right woman. That way it only makes sense that they combine houses into his already snug and perfect little cottage."

This time Charles's laugh was a bellow.

"You know—" Georgette mused, nibbling her bottom lip, "—if we found a place like ours."

"Far too large for him."

"No, I mean a place that needs a little work. A place that you can get for a song—"

Charles glanced at her. "You're serious?"

"Of course I am. You're happier when your nephews

are around, Charles. I want you to be happy. I'm going to talk to Barnaby about it. He knows everyone."

"This is for me?" Charles sounded surprised.

"Surely you know that when I gave you my heart," Georgette told him, pulling his hand towards her and kissing one of his knuckles, "that meant that you got all of my machinations, conniving, and loving on your behalf. Besides—I'd prefer the village's attention turn from me to the newest Mrs. Aaron. Surely, Robert will marry a flashy bright young thing who will draw all eyes. I can fade again."

"Oh ho—" Charles laughed, re-tangling their fingers together. "None of that, Mrs. Aaron. I'm afraid you've been outed."

"No," Georgette disagreed, shaking her head. She leaned towards him as if she were telling him a secret and whispered. "Did you know? I find that I really don't like very many people."

Charles was putting the auto in park when she said that, so the burst of laughter didn't end them in a ditch, but Georgette abandoned him to guffaws and let the dogs out of the auto. She glanced back at him as she moseyed towards the house and saw the happiness on his face. There was a clear glint of appreciation in his eyes as he paced after her.

Charles was, to be sure, very handsome. Or maybe that was her vision of him. She saw him through a gaze of love. He was, certainly, distinguished. His dark hair was edged with grey at the temples, but it only seemed to add to his looks. He wasn't a particularly large man either in height or strength, but he was strong enough and tall enough for her.

He was the kind of man who didn't turn heads, but somehow he'd had a whole slew of women wanting him. He had, very clearly, been the one who'd noticed her and loved her first. The idea that when a man was downright pursued by a drove of debutantes—well-off ones at that— and still looked about the world and wanted the plain Georgette Dorothy Marsh showed that Charles Aaron was a man of odd tastes.

He said that she was lovely, but she didn't really believe it. She was fine enough, she supposed. Decent, but unremarkable. She was neither tall nor short. She was neither dark nor fair. The most appropriate term for her was medium. No. Middling. She was middling.

"I know that look—" He had the expression of a man who had told her that she was perfect and not been believed too many times. "You're perfect."

Georgette glanced at him and then bypassed the front doors to take the dogs around the back of the house. They followed faithfully and sniffed around as she found a cushiony patch of clover to sit before recalling how wet it would be. Charles, however, must have divined her intent because he joined her with a thick blanket that he spread on the ground.

They sat and the dogs hurried to climb into her lap. They had to scrabble over each other, rather like goats shoving each other off the mound in order to be the king of the mountain. Georgette let them lick her as they struggled to get closer until they finally settled in happily, one dog on Charles's lap with Dorcas and Susan on her own.

"I want to visit the new doctor," Georgette told him, "and check in on the poor attacked woman."

"You're curious."

She grinned and admitted, "Perhaps. But I'd have checked on Katherine's daughter-in-law regardless. I'll be checking in on Katherine as well."

Georgette laid her head against his shoulder. He sighed for them both. "Why on earth would anyone attack a middle-aged woman in the middle of the wood near her mother-in-law's house? It's just—unthinkable."

Georgette didn't have the answer, but she very much expected that whatever the reason, it wouldn't be good enough. Why would someone kill another over the contents of a book? Why would a woman blackmail her long-time friend? Why would a man who supposedly loved you, kill you if you rejected a proposal? She had met people who had done all of those things, and yet—she still didn't understand.

Charles turned her face towards his and laid a fervent kiss on her lips before he said, "They're probably wondering where we are. I'll work from home tomorrow, shall I?"

She didn't argue because she knew he wouldn't leave her regardless. Instead she said, "We could visit the new doctor and take Lucy with us to get Janey. Perhaps we could go to the pictures and enjoy the day. Janey wants to see Snow White and the Seven Dwarves desperately, and the theater is playing it near her school."

Charles nodded and rose, shooing the dogs away. He pulled Georgette to her feet and shook out the blanket, and then led the way inside. Georgette avoided Eunice and the kitchen. There was no way that Georgette's long-time helper would avoid scolding her thoroughly for finding another victim.

Georgette considered avoiding supper entirely, but she knew she'd never get away with it. There was a moment of feeling rather suffocated. If this were a little more than a year ago, Georgette would have been able to go to bed early with a cup of tea and a book. Now, she had to do things like check on Lucy, let Charles ensure she ate enough for their baby, and then fall asleep in his arms. All good things, she reminded herself, escaping into their bathroom to the claw-foot tub that would let her sink low. She didn't need to be dressed for dinner for at least an hour and soaking in lavender bath salts might be enough.

As soon as she was alone, her mind turned back to the woman. Had the wind picked up first or the sound she heard? Were they connected? Surely there would have been a scream if it were an attack?

Unless, whoever had struck her down had crept up behind her. How horrifying. Maybe the woman had been stretching her legs in her mother-in-law's garden and then been struck down by a passerby.

But that didn't strike Georgette as likely. Why would someone find Katherine's house, which was off the beaten path, and then attack a woman in the orchard? What if— what if the woman had been cut down by someone she knew? What if the woman had been walking with another person and then been attacked in a rage? It made an unfortunate amount of sense to Georgette, but the equivalent would be Georgette being struck down by Charles or Eunice or Marian or Lucy. The idea made Georgette shiver despite the hot water. She got out of the bath, having lost the relaxing nature of the lavender salts.

❧   4   ❧

CHARLES AARON

Charles expected Georgette to take a bath and he relaxed at the sound of the water and then left their bedroom for the office. He knew he was too worried over her with their baby. It was only that he hadn't expected to be quite so happy in their marriage, and carrying and giving birth to a child was a dangerous endeavor.

Charles found Joseph in his office when he entered and the two of them looked at each other.

"Your pretending it wasn't serious didn't work."

Joseph shook his head. "You should have known it wouldn't. Georgie is way too smart for that, and who can gloss over a woman with a wound on the back of her head and a broken fence post nearby? The thing was bloody, Charles."

Charles sighed as he leaned back in chair, reaching for the decanter and two glasses on the small table behind his desk. Joseph poured the brandy while Charles lit his pipe. "What happened?"

"She's not awake yet. Dr. West said we won't know if she's going to be all right until she does. We have the bloody fence post, which is obviously the weapon used on the woman, but there doesn't seem to be anything else to find. Georgette didn't see anything. No one else was near. The constable sent for Katherine Lynd. Perhaps she will know something. But so far, we're paused."

Charles sighed. "What are the chances that Georgette is in danger?"

"Slim, I'd think. The dogs were barking when she approached. It would have warned off whoever hit the woman. He's going to know that he's safe since we haven't come for him."

Charles wasn't comforted. He rubbed the back of his neck as he considered. After the events with Dr. Fowler, Charles had changed the locks on the house, both doors and windows. He wasn't going to have another man entering his house easily and send Georgette running for her life. Not again.

"Being in love is stressful," Joseph told Charles, lighting his cigarette and then glancing at his uncle. "Marian's family is driving me mad."

Charles puffed on his pipe. "Is Marian arriving?"

Joseph shook his head. "Her mother wanted Marian to accompany her to something or other. Do you know—" Joseph snapped his mouth shut, took a sip of his brandy, and then added, "Do you know I told her family that I wasn't going to be able to come to dinner two days ago. I stopped by after to see if she wanted to walk. They had a fellow there."

"A fellow?" Charles sipped his own brandy, suspecting he'd need it before Joseph finished.

"A young law school graduate. Handsome. Rich."

Charles refilled Joseph's glass in answer.

"Marian was laughing."

"Georgette swears she loves you."

"Her mother doesn't," Joseph grumbled and then swallowed a large drink. "I think that might matter more."

GEORGETTE DOROTHY AARON

The next morning, Charles had slept longer and later since he wasn't going into the office. When Georgette woke, one of his arms was still under her cheek while the other rested across her hip. She breathed in slowly and realized he wasn't sleeping.

She opened her eyes and found that he was staring at her. "That's spooky."

"Me watching you?"

She nodded and he grinned. He pressed a kiss on her forehead then said, "I suppose you'll be dragging me through the village today."

"You don't have to come."

"There's a special kind of pleasure in watching you interact with the world."

She frowned at the glint of humor in his eyes and then turned onto her back, stretching out her toes. She left him in the bed and went to wash her face and brush her teeth and dress. For visiting the local surgery on an early autumn day, Georgette chose a light blue dress, a cardigan, and a sturdy pair of shoes. Topped with her coat and hat, she'd be quite respectable enough.

When she found Charles in the breakfast room, Joseph had joined them from his cottage, Lucy was actually in attendance, and Eunice had lingered. She hadn't been merciful either. There were poached eggs, bacon, sausages, and a glint in her gaze that dared Georgette to object.

"Well?" Eunice demanded without preamble. "What have you to say for yourself? What happened?"

"I saw nothing but a bloody branch."

"Why didn't you come back here instead of to the Mustly's?" Eunice sniffed and then made Georgette toast, shoving it in front of her. "You need to eat. What happened?"

Georgette frowned. She didn't enjoy mornings and she enjoyed them even less when Eunice was both angry and protective. Georgette was never prepared for that level of interaction before at least two cups of tea.

"You'd gone before I left," Georgette told Eunice, striving and failing at a patient tone. "I'd have asked you to go with me if you were here. I knew that Anna and Barnaby would be home. And I knew that Anna could show the constable where we were and that I could take Barnaby with me, so I wasn't alone with whatever had happened. At the time, I thought it was all a rather horrible accident and that the woman was in need of immediate help."

Georgette closed her eyes against all of the gazes on

her. She said, trying again for patience and possibly succeeding, "I saw nothing. I found the woman because Susan was upset and led me there. She let out quite a ruckus. The only thing Barnaby and I saw out of place was one bloody piece of wood."

Georgette ate quietly and they let her, to her utter relief. When she rose, however, Charles rose with her. "Shall we go for a walk?"

Georgette eyed him sideways.

"I know you'll be visiting the woman at the doctor's surgery and Katherine," he said, "and I'd rather do that with you."

Charles gathered their coats while Georgette placed her hat on her head and pinned it into place. When she stepped out onto the walk with her dogs, Charles stepped out beside her. "Inside."

Susan whined while Dorcas let out a mournful moan.

"Inside," Charles commanded, and all three dogs returned inside, glancing back, as they walked as slowly as possible. Charles closed the door and held out his arm. The two of them walked along the river after they'd reached the end of their street. The doctor had not taken the same place as Dr. Fowler, but Joseph had discovered the location the previous day. It was a small storefront with a set of rooms overhead and the new doctor had taken both.

When they reached the door, they found a simple name in block writing, 'Dr. Nathaniel West,' on the door and nothing else. The bell above the door rang as they entered, and they stared around the waiting room. There was an unattended desk, several comfortable chairs that were empty, and from behind a swinging door—the man appeared.

Georgette had seen him the day before, but she'd been too distracted to take note. He was young. He seemed barely older than their Eddie who was merely 16 years old. Even if this fellow had graduated already, he must be in his mid-twenties. He certainly didn't look like it. His ears stuck out a little, and he was very thin, with spots on his chin, and a suit that looked like a costume. But when he introduced himself, his gaze was alert and active with an air of intelligence that startled Georgette.

"Are you Mrs. Lynd's family?"

Georgette shook her head. "Did she wake?"

"Just this morning," Dr. West said, holding out his hand. "Dr. Nathaniel West."

Charles answered while Georgette glanced around, noting the utter lack of evidence that the young doctor had any patients. Would anyone come to see someone who looked to be an age with one of the schoolboys?

Georgette asked him, "Is Katherine Lynd here?"

The doctor shook his head, explaining, "She stayed rather late last night and said she'd be back this morning, but she's yet to appear. Her son, the patient's husband, hadn't arrived by the time I had to close the surgery."

Georgette nodded. She bypassed the doctor, ignoring his objections as she stepped into the room with a hospital bed. "Hello."

The woman looked up and scowled. She was a large woman, with thick forearms that proclaimed a life of labor. Her cheeks were ruddy with very pale skin around the edges and watery blue eyes. Her frown was deep, and

Georgette had to wonder if the victim were so unappealing because of the frown or was she just naturally that way.

"I should have guessed you wouldn't be Katherine. I'm entirely unsurprised to be alone and bereft."

"Oh?" Bereft?

"She's probably lingering over her cats or harvesting her flowers. She doesn't care about me."

Georgette lifted her brows and glanced back, but Charles hadn't followed. Georgette took the seat next to the bed and introduced herself. "What were you doing at Katherine's home?"

"What were you doing there?"

Georgette leaned back. "I was attempting to visit my friend."

"I was visiting my mother-in-law. Though why I bother, I do not know."

Georgette could see why Katherine hadn't arrived yet. She was a good woman, but anyone would lose patience with this vitriol. Perhaps, however, it was the result of being quite so uncomfortable. That knock on the back of her head couldn't have felt good.

"Did you want some water?"

"The doctor wants me to wait to eat or drink." The woman said it as though Dr. West was torturing her for the joy of it.

Georgette sighed and then asked, "Is there anything that could make you more comfortable?"

"My husband. My family." She frowned. "What was your name again?"

"Georgette Aaron. And you?"

"Lizette Lynd."

Georgette offered to fluff her pillows and was declined. She offered to get her a blanket and got a dark look and a comment on the stuffiness. "It wouldn't have killed that child pretending to be a doctor to crack a window."

"Do you remember anything?" Georgette asked, finished with offering kindness and receiving sourness.

Lizette scoffed. "Are you a police officer?"

"Just a concerned local."

"Then mind your own business."

Georgette took in a deep breath, held it, and then answered, "I'm delighted to see you're awake. I was quite worried when I ran myself sick through the wood to get you help. I'll stop by later and see if you need anything."

Lizette didn't even seem bothered by Georgette's insinuation. Perhaps all of mankind was expected to jump to her assistance. Georgette shook her head. She'd have expected someone to do the same for her if she'd been found hurt in a wood, though she would have been grateful afterwards, but she wouldn't begrudge her own actions simply because Lizette's gaze was narrowed on Georgette like she had stepped in feces.

Georgette left quickly and found Dr. West and Charles near the receptionist desk. "You have your hands full, Dr. West."

His ears turned red, but beyond that reaction, he revealed nothing else. "We are often not ourselves when we're poorly."

Georgette smiled at him, surprised again. "Too true, doctor. When did you move to our little village?"

"Only a week ago."

Georgette felt the need to invite him to dinner, fought it, and lost. "How lovely to have you here. Would you like to join us for supper on Sunday? We're new ourselves and it's good to know a few faces."

"Oh yes!"

The doctor accepted so quickly, Georgette wondered if he wasn't a bit lonely. She glanced at Charles who stepped in and said their goodbyes.

"Darling Georgette," he began after they had left. Of course he'd seen her conflicted thoughts. "You'd rather have dinner alone in bed than entertain the doctor."

"I know!"

"Yet long-ago manners drilled into the younger you, ignored for years and now revived, insisted that you invite him to our house."

"I know!" Georgette pressed her cheek into Charles's shoulder and whined, "I don't know what is wrong with me. The best that can be said is that at least it'll be in the comfort of our own home rather than being stuck in some...some...grumpy housewife's dinner party who is competing against a standard we know nothing about."

Charles's laugh was not at all commiserating. "You say that as though there are secret wars between the house-wives of Harper's Hollow."

Georgette lifted a brow at him and shook her head. "Charles darling," she mocked sarcastically. "There is nothing to be said other than you know not of what you speak."

"Oh, really?" His tone demanded an explanation.

"Longtime bachelors know nothing of the troubles of a small-town woman in a time of struggle. You and I are blessed with an excess in a time of struggle. So many aren't. It's hard enough to be a wife and a mother when you aren't begging for the scraps of someone else's rejected cabbages and gleaning the fields to feed too many children."

"I know, darling. I'm sorry."

"That's not what I'm saying. We're blessed more than most, Charles. You have your work and I have my writing, and we don't find our importance by serving the best tea or being the one who engineers things for the school. Charles, the world of a housewife is so often so small that there are utter battles over being the one who makes the best fruitcake, puts together the church's flowers, or wins the ribbons at the fair."

"Are there really?" It was clear the idea had never occurred to him.

Georgette nodded, feeling a surprising sorrow for those women. Not because their worlds were small. Many of them gloried in their roles. She was sorry for the one who were suffocating slowly. Georgette didn't know how they felt, though not because she hadn't been suffocating before her book was published. She had been.

She had discovered by writing she had something to offer. Before then, she had been suffocating differently. Not lost in a family with too many mouths, not enough money, and a struggling world. She'd suffered almost entirely alone. Unwanted. Unseen. A housewife with children could easily be drowning surrounded by those who loved her.

She shivered at the thought and the shadows of her own memories and turned to Charles. He had been, after all, the first person to notice she was a person. "I love you rather desperately, Mr. Aaron."

"Then we're in agreement, Mrs. Aaron, for I have found that I am rather lost without you."

He tugged her into a shadow of a hedge, took her face between his hands, and his next response was given with his lips, his hands, and their exchange of breath.

❦ 5 ❦

JOSEPH AARON

Joseph walked to meet the early train on the off chance that Marian would get off. She usually came to Harper's Hollow to stay with Georgette on Thursday nights. Marian preferred to be in attendance when Janey came back from school. The two of them, with little Janey, tended towards long walks, conversation over Georgette's writing, and for a while—imagining the cottage that Joseph had bought for Marian together.

Marian's joy in the cottage had been lost in the last weeks. The light in her eyes as he approached had gone out, and he was rather afraid that he should offer to let her out of their engagement. The sheer idea of it, however, left him rebelling. No. If she wanted to throw him over and give his ring back, he wasn't going to make it easier for her.

Joseph took his auto to the doctor's office. He'd heard at the pub there was a new doctor in the village and laughed along with the bartender about the baby-faced fool who thought he could build a business here. Joseph had suggested the man might have thought he'd have a better chance in a place where the last doctor had been a killer—and a fool.

Joseph found the doctor's office and noticed Georgette and Charles walking down the street. They turned into the teashop before Joseph stepped into the doctor's office. He'd met the fellow the night before when he'd been turned away from the woman—who had after all not even woken up yet.

"Hello doctor," Joseph said, holding out his hand and shaking the other fellow's. "How's the patient?"

"A bit sour, I'm afraid."

"Doctor!" a woman's voice snapped. "Doctor! Are you even here?" The sound of dark muttering extended to the office and the poor man clenched his jaw.

"You've your hands full," Joseph said.

"That's what Mrs. Aaron said."

The woman in the back room shouted, "Is it a party out there? Where is my mother-in-law? Typical, of course, that I'm discarded and alone after being hurt. Doctor! Doctor! I say, doctor! If you think I'm paying for this utter abandonment, you are very wrong sir! Doctor!"

"I'll go ahead, shall I?" Joseph said, slapping the doctor on the back.

"I won't pretend I'm not relieved," Dr. West said, shaking his head. "She's a fierce one."

Joseph nodded. "Take a chance for coffee or tea, my friend. This isn't my field, and I have no intention of staying, and I'll be leaving as soon as I get the information I need."

"I need help," Dr. West muttered. "I need an assistant."

Joseph snorted and left, finding his way to the room where Lizette Lynd was sitting up, picking at her blanket. It wasn't plain and utilitarian but looked like a quilt from the doctor's own bed.

"Can you believe this place?" she snapped. "Who are you? Where is my husband? Where is my mother-in-law?"

"They were here quite late, ma'am," Joseph told her. "I took them both home very early this morning."

Lizette Lynd scoffed. "I shouldn't be here alone." She sniffed, glancing him up and down, and then ordered, "Go get them."

Joseph took a seat.

"I said to go get them."

"I'm not your servant, Mrs. Lynd. I'm a Detective Inspector for Scotland Yard, and I'm here to find out what happened."

Mrs. Lynd's pale blue eyes sharpened and her face blanked. Joseph stared in a bit of shock as the woman overtly crossed her arms over her chest. "I have no intention of answering questions without my husband present. In fact, I am quite uncomfortable by your presence in my room."

Joseph blinked. Her accusation was dark enough that he knew he'd be accused of something untoward if he didn't leave immediately. There was a cleared throat near the doorway and Joseph glanced back and saw Dr. West.

"That's quite enough of that, Mrs. Lynd," Dr. West said. "You aren't alone or being molested."

Mrs. Lynd eyes widened and her face flushed. She opened her mouth to let out what would, no doubt, be a tirade.

Joseph jumped in. "Who hurt you, Mrs. Lynd?"

She shook her head.

"Did you see them?

She shook her head.

"Who knew you were at your mother-in-law's?"

Lizette Lynd lifted her eyebrows and shook her head.

"Mrs. Lynd, I need answers or I'm going to assume you're protecting someone. Your husband perhaps?"

Joseph could well imagine knocking this woman a good one over the back of her head. Being married to her? That sourness being your regular good morning? Joseph shook his head. "You need to answer these questions, Mrs. Lynd. If it wasn't anyone you know, if we have a rampaging criminal on our hands and they hurt another when you refused to answer? Well now—that comes back to you."

It was the wrong thing to say. She leaned back, closed her eyes, and said, "Dr. West, I feel quite ill."

The two men looked at each other and then Dr. West jerked his head towards the door of the room. They walked out together.

"I could use a drink," Dr. West muttered.

"I'll buy you one when this is over," Joseph said. "And I think I have an idea of who can help you in the short term. Let me find Georgette."

"Mrs. Aaron? Her husband seems too protective of her to allow her to work here."

"Oh, Georgette is too busy, and Charles would never be happy with Georgette being run off her feet by that

Mrs. Lynd. They know a person. Let me talk to Georgette and have her ask the girl I'm thinking of." Joseph slapped Dr. West on the back again. "I'll go offer Mrs. Lynd and her son a ride to your office and then see what else can be done."

Joseph would have admitted to fleeing into the nighttime, but it was mid-morning. He crossed to his auto and then realized that Katherine Lynd and her son were approaching. He'd met Mrs. Lynd at Georgette's during tea a time or two, but the previous night was the first time he'd met the son. John Lynd was a big man. He had large brown eyes with dark circles under them, and a big belly. Before he'd realized how hurt his wife had been, he'd seemed jolly.

The fellow had deflated when he'd seen his wife. He'd taken her hand. "Zette? Zettie, darling? Please." He'd collapsed into the chair next to his wife with his mother rubbing his back. "Please, sweetheart. Please."

Joseph shook his head and then reached out. "Good news, John, your wife is awake and talking."

"Thank god," he said. "She must be sassy since we're late. Mother—"

"She'll understand," Katherine told him, her gaze darting to Joseph and then back to her son. This was not a woman who believed what she was saying. "We can only do what we can do, John."

John nodded and hurried towards the doctor's office while Katherine stayed behind.

"John wasn't here with her yesterday," she told Joseph quietly.

"How do you know?" Joseph asked.

Katherine glanced behind her, making sure that her

son wasn't around and then told him. "I'm aware of what my daughter-in-law is."

Joseph lifted his brows.

"My son has loved her since he was thirteen years old." She shook her head and added, "I don't know why."

Joseph had no idea what to say to that. His eyes landed on a lovely, young woman, slender and perfect who had him completely besotted. He wanted to cross to her, but he couldn't leave the interview. He tried to nod at her, but he could see immediately that in not crossing to her, he'd made a mistake.

Marian shook her head at him and turned towards Georgette's house. But first, she stared a long time at the leaving train. The next was a few hours away, and she couldn't escape him.

"Do you know who would have hurt her?"

Katherine paused. Joseph suspected that she might have had an answer, but it would include many of the people she loved. Instead she shook her head again and told Joseph, "I'm needed inside."

By the time Mrs. Lynd had stepped away from him, Marian was gone. Joseph considered going back to the scene of the crime, but what he needed was a person who had an idea of the vagaries of the Lynd family. Joseph guessed who might be able to help, but he'd be damned if he didn't go chasing after Marian.

He ran down the street after her and called, "Marian?"

If she heard him, she didn't reply. He shouldn't have been so upset about that fellow at her family dinner. But —he couldn't help it. He knew her parents were trying to talk her out of marrying him, but he knew that he could trust her. However, there was a pit growing in his stomach that he was going to lose her all the same.

What he needed, he thought, was Georgette on his side. Georgette's opinion was the most important to Marian. If Joseph were being honest with himself, he'd admit that he was jealous. Was his jealousy why things were going so wrong with Marian? He shook his head as he tried the teashop. He wanted to talk to people who he respected and trusted, but Georgette and Charles had left. The vicar's wife was nearby, but she wouldn't do.

❧ 6 ☙

GEORGETTE DOROTHY AARON

Georgette had decided to look for Joseph when Joseph found her. He looked at her for a long moment and then collapsed into one of the chairs in her office and admitted, "I'm messing everything up with Marian and I don't know what to do."

She stared at him, surprised and then asked quietly. "Why are you telling me?"

"Georgette," he laughed weakly, "the look on your face." He shook his head and then took a seat next to her typewriter. "I'm asking you because you're the matriarch now."

"The what?" She knew she was staring, but she couldn't stop herself. She must be gaping like a fish, mouth open, eyes wide, suffocating by the sheer idea of anyone looking to her for anything other than an odd tea.

She poured herself a fortifying cuppa, added an excess

of milk, and then added a further excess of sugar. She closed her eyes as she sipped it and then cast a daggered glance at Joseph.

"I am not the matriarch."

"Charles is the patriarch."

She tried intensifying the daggered glance, but he only laughed at her.

"Would you deny us a mother?" he tried and Georgette winced.

"I believe that we're of a similar age, Joseph."

"Do you know what I remember about my mother?" He didn't wait for her answer. "Her smell. The tone of her voice. The way she always made sure I was all right. Even when I wasn't all right, I'd talk to her and then it would be okay."

"Are you not all right, Joseph?"

He shook his head. "I'm not. I—Marian's family hates me."

Georgette's eyes widened and she put her cup of tea in front of her mouth.

"Hiding your reaction doesn't change the facts, Georgette. Her family hates me."

"They're concerned," she said carefully. "Being married to a Scotland Yard man can be a hard life, Joseph. You work long, odd hours. She'll be alone quite often. Her parents do have valid concerns, and you know they are right to."

He put his hands over his face. "So I should be unhappy? She knew what I was when I pursued her, Georgette."

Georgette bit down on her bottom lip, fighting the desire to spew her thoughts. She couldn't betray Marian's confidences despite any burning desire to leap into the fray and fix things between the first and best of her friends and her new family.

Georgette took in a deep breath. "What I needed from Charles was his honesty."

"My honesty is that her parents are driving me mad, they're trying to control her, and it infuriates me. How am I supposed to tell her that I'm growing to despise them?"

"You despise my family?" Marian asked from the doorway. She had been upset since she'd arrived, but now she was pale, red circles on her cheeks, dark circles under her eyes.

Joseph's reply was a dark curse. "Damn it, Georgette!"

"It's not her fault that you have secrets about my family!" Marian clutched her collarbone and a tear ran down her cheek. "Joseph—" She stopped with a choked cry and ran from the room.

Georgette carefully crossed her fingers and studied him. "Are you going to go after her?"

"No!" He cursed again. "No, I have to work, Georgette. I—the doctor needs help with that woman there. What do you think of sending Lucy?"

Georgette blinked in surprise and then said, "I suppose you should ask her. Make sure you tell Lucy that the woman is sour before you start pitching charity at her. She wants to help."

"I will." He sighed. He stood and then said, "If my loving Marian matters, help me, please. Surely being loved and wanted is of a value of itself? No man is going to be perfect."

Georgette squeezed his hand, but she didn't make a promise. She wasn't sure she could. The look on Marian's face—it had been painful to see. Things were going wrong between Marian and Joseph, and Georgette was afraid to make it worse.

He searched her face and accepted what he saw there. "I need to talk to someone about Katherine's family. Lizette is giving us nothing. She refused to answer my questions and instead insinuated that I was abusing her."

Georgette frowned. "Did you get assigned to this case?"

"They asked, I live here, it's an easy request to answer. Especially since I'm in between larger cases. I think my supervisor thought it would take an afternoon. Who would guess that the victim would refuse to answer questions?"

"I've been thinking about that," Georgette mused.

Georgette paused long enough to see what he'd say, but he only waited for her to continue.

"She's a mean woman. I could imagine that a passerby attacked her."

"In Harper's Hollow? Off the beaten path? With no tramps around? I suppose it's possible a person came through, but these fellows are looking for work, not someone to attack."

"There are more tramps lately." Georgette's doubt filled her tone and Joseph nodded. "There are so many people who don't have enough. Under enough provoca-tion, one might lash out at a woman, especially a scornful one like Mrs. Lynd."

Joseph shook his head, not that Georgette was wrong. It was that neither of them believed that a random person found Lizette Lynd in the wood and decided to strike her down no matter how ugly she'd behaved. It was possible, but likely? No. Georgette didn't believe it.

Especially since there hadn't been a rumor of tramps seen wandering the village. It was incredibly unlikely that a stranger was seen in the village on the same day that a woman was struck down, and they wouldn't hear of it a good half-dozen times before the day was over.

"If it isn't a stranger," Georgette said, "the person who tried to hurt Lizette Lynd knows her, knows Katherine's home, and knew that Lizette could be found there."

Joseph said nothing, but she knew he agreed. There was, after all, a reason he was looking into Katherine's family.

"Higgins is doing the rounds. Questioning those who spend time in the wood or were in it yesterday, but so far no one has seen anything."

"Anna Mustly is who you want to talk to," Georgette told him. "She knows Katherine well. In fact, it was Anna who walked me over to meet Katherine the first time."

Joseph nodded and started to leave. He looked back to Georgette and added, "It wouldn't be a bad idea for you to avoid the wood until we're sure."

❧

GEORGETTE WATCHED MARIAN FROM THE DOORWAY OF her bedroom for a long time before she said, "Hello darling."

Marian looked up from the window and wiped her tears away. "Hello darling."

The repeated phrase was darker and cracked when Marian said it. Georgette sat down next to her friend on the window seat and wrapped her arm around the younger woman. "Shall we dip into Charles's bar and have cocktails?"

"It isn't even teatime."

"You know I do appreciate a good afternoon tea and some deep breaths, but we can give your tea a little extra zazzle."

Marian laughed a woeful sound. Her gaze met Georgette's and she sniffed, pressing her finger against the corner of her eye to dab away another tear. "Will you still love me if Joseph and I don't work out?"

Just saying the words had Marian collapsing into her handkerchief.

"You know what I hear when you weep like that?"

Marian shook her head, still curled into her hands and handkerchief.

"That you love him."

Marian didn't reply and Georgette bit down on her bottom lip to prevent herself from demanding an answer. Instead she looked out the window where Marian had been staring and saw Joseph talking with Anna Mustly in the back garden.

Oh, Marian, Georgette thought, and then said, "I was going to go to the baker and the grocer and see if I can bring a few things to Katherine's family. Eunice is making them a meal that they can heat as they choose, but I thought it might be nice to get a few things that were a bit easier. Perhaps fruit and bread?"

Marian sniffed, blew her nose, and said, "Let me wash my face. Fresh air would do me good." She shivered as though her lungs and body fought against calm.

Georgette watched Marian disappear into the bath

and then wondered if it would be too obvious to walk to the main part of the village by way of the cottage Joseph had bought for Marian.

Marian grabbed a jumper, slid it over the top of her dress, brushed her hair, and then asked, "Do I look like I was crying?"

Georgette refrained from cursing her lightly. Was she red-nosed, blotchy-faced, swollen, and somehow both pale and heated? No. She looked slightly red around the eyes and flushed on her cheeks, drawing attention to her overall beauty. Georgette on the other hand, fit the first description when she truly cried.

"You look lovely," Georgette said sourly. Since they'd had the conversation about their respective looks when weeping, Marian laughed as they stepped out onto the landing.

Joseph had reached the door to Charles's office and looked up. Seeing Marian grinning seemed to wound him, but Marian only saw the dark look he cast at her.

"Did you see how he looked at me?" Marian whispered. "If looks could kill, he'd have just murdered me."

Georgette considered and abandoned several replies and then it was too late.

The two friends made their way to the kitchens where Eunice was cooking two dinners.

"Hello darling, Eunice," Georgette said, kissing her cheek. "Do you have a list of things we should acquire for Katherine and her family?"

Eunice nodded towards the end of the counter, and Georgette picked up the sheet of paper. Eunice glanced at Marian and then lifted a brow. "Fighting with Joseph again?"

"I think it's all falling apart," Marian wailed and then took in a deep breath, screwing her eyes shut.

"And I thought you were stupid when it came to Charles," Eunice told Georgette flatly, entirely without sympathy. "Use your eyes, Marian. Stop listening to all the poison."

"Is that what he said?" Marian demanded, eyes suddenly flashing with fury.

"That's what you said," Eunice replied. Marian stepped back, shocked, and Eunice took the chance to turn to Georgette. "Lucy went to help the doctor. He's very grateful, but Charles told her she can't stay overnight. I volunteered to do so instead. If you don't need me?"

"That's very kind of you," Georgette said carefully. "Perhaps someone from Katherine's family would be a better choice than you, darling."

Eunice laughed low and said, "The doctor needs a person who isn't used to obeying when that woman says jump. I heard about her from Charles, Joseph, and Anna. She sounds like she's a handful."

Georgette opened the back door to prevent Marian from getting up in arms again as she had that look about her. Was she fleeing? Georgette had to admit she was. She was growing tired of confrontation.

Marian's cottage was the closet to the village and the dogs were used to the walk, so the four of them, Georgette's three and Marion's one, surged ahead. It would probably be faster to go that way, but Georgette saw the sick look on Marian's face.

No, Georgette thought, her friend wouldn't find her way while she was being assaulted on every side. Instead, she called the dogs back and then said to Marian, "Shall we take the auto? That way we won't have to carry every-thing over the hill and through the woods."

Marian's agreement was pure relief, and Georgette hooked her arm through Marian's.

"I love you, my dear friend."

"Even without Joseph?"

"I know you love him, as angry as you are," Georgette said gently. "So, I will hope and pray for a happily ever after instead. But regardless of that fate—you are my dearest friend and I will love you to the end of time."

Marian nodded, but she wasn't any more relieved.

"Did you want to tell me about it?"

Marian shook her head and then whispered, "Not yet. I will."

⚜ 7 ⚜

GEORGETTE DOROTHY AARON

nna Mustly saw them getting into the auto and called, "Oh! Do you mind if I ride with you? Barnaby has gone out with the constables and I would like to bring a little something to Katherine. Is that where you're going?"

Georgette nodded. She glanced at Marian who seemed to be relieved to open the back door and get into the back of the auto instead. The dogs barked and Georgette clucked, letting all four of them get into the back of the auto with Marian. What was better than the unconditional adoration of furry little friends? Between Marian's own dog and Georgette's three, Marian might feel all right again by the time they reached the village.

"We're going to the grocer and baker first," Georgette told Anna. "Then back here to get Eunice's dinner for them. Then to Katherine's to deliver."

Anna noted the look on Marian's face and asked, "I don't mind running errands with you if you are certain you don't mind if I come along." It was apparent she regretted asking, looking at the tear stains that hadn't faded yet.

"A little distraction is a good thing," Marian said, avoiding everyone's gaze.

Georgette nodded and gestured to Anna to join them.

"Tell me about Katherine's family," Georgette suggested. "I know she has at least one daughter and a few sons, but I can't remember the details. Other than the son and daughter-in-law I've met, of course."

Anna looked over and winced a little. "Katherine talks about her daughter the most. Emmanuline looks after her mother more carefully than the other children. But, Katherine has four sons along with Emmanuline."

"Five children!" Georgette tried to imagine it, but she couldn't quite envision such a thing. She was an only child. How wonderful would it have been to not be alone all these years after her parents died?

Anna continued. "Katherine's oldest is John. Next is Mitchell, then Brent, then Jedediah. Emmanuline is the baby. Mitchell is quite a successful banker, Brent is a bit of a rebel, but he works on fishing boats and does all right. Jedediah has a little farm not too far away. John and Jedediah both work in the village over. John worked on autos, trucks, and airplanes in the Great War. When he came home, he opened a garage. Only—"

"Only?" Marian asked, sounding intrigued. Good, Georgette thought, it was important to get lost in other people's stories. Sometimes seeing the goods and the bads of other lives helped you appreciate your own.

"He was injured a few years back. It's hard enough with people trying to pay with chicken eggs and potatoes if they can. John is a softie, he takes payment in trade, lets people who owe him money miss payments. Lizette doesn't have the same kindness."

Georgette nibbled her thumb as she considered. Impossible. A kind man who struggled to survive unable to say no to those who were also struggling married to a harridan. Something had to give. Perhaps it was one of those who owed him money who'd attacked his wife. Maybe she'd demanded payment and they hadn't been able to pay? Maybe she'd demanded another form of payment? Georgette couldn't imagine what.

"Why don't we see them more often?" Marian asked. "I'm here most weekends and Katherine never has her children around."

Anna's mouth twisted. "Lizette mostly. She insists that every family dinner be where she is. It's easier for Katherine to travel, Lizette claims. Most of them comply with whatever Lizette wants to keep the peace."

Georgette winced. She'd heard Katherine say many times how she'd raised her children, imagining her grand-children walking where her children walked. It was a shame that those things didn't happen very often. It wasn't, however, a reason you struck another down over.

"That's what my family is like," Marian said. "My siblings and I comply with our parents to avoid the conflict."

Anna and Georgette needed to be congratulated for not meeting each other's gazes. Instead, Anna turned behind her to Marian and said, "I've long been of the opinion that we only have one life to live."

Georgette could imagine that Marian was wondering what that meant, but she didn't ask further questions.

Anna, however, didn't let it lie. "Why would you let anyone else live yours too? There's a point where the elders in our lives or our smarter siblings or whoever it is that is trying to rule our lives is simply an autocrat. You have one life to live, so don't let someone else live it."

"How do you know what to do?" Marian asked softly.

"You have to set aside all the conflicting voices and decide what you want. What you truly want."

"But what if what you want has a price you don't want to pay?"

"Then you have to decide if that price is worth more or less than the thing you want. In the end, which choice will you regret the most?"

Marian didn't say anything else and Georgette didn't really feel like she could comment. She hadn't had to choose between family and love. It was odd for her to listen to this. It didn't trigger her empathy. If anything, Georgette felt irritated, but she didn't want to be that person.

She hadn't had the luxury of an opinionated family who cared about her choices. Which wasn't to say that Georgette didn't have an opinion. She did. She thought that Marian's family needed to let Marian live her own life. It wasn't as if Joseph were cruel or married or far, far too old for Marian. Joseph was, indisputably, a good man who was trying to make Marian happy.

On the other hand, Georgette's parents lived in her heart, but the days of the clarity of memory regarding them were gone. What would Georgette give to have another day with her mother? To refresh her mind on how mother had smelled and spoke? Georgette hadn't had the wisdom to ask many of her questions before her mother and father had died. She had thought she'd had more time, and she'd been wrong.

What would Georgette hand over, what price would she pay to have a cup of tea and tell Mum that a grandbaby was on the way? To simply spend a day sipping tea and chatting idly as they had over every holiday? To make a chocolate cake together and dip into the frosting as they laughed? What would she give to wrap her baby in a blanket that had been knitted by a grandmother?

Georgette gripped the steering wheel and commented on the lingering flowers in Anna's garden. She wasn't sure that she could handle any of this. Georgette was emotional since realizing she was carrying a baby. Whatever it was about being with child, it left one prone to tears and—perhaps—a touch of madness. There was a piece of herself that she was trying to bury deep that was seething with jealousy of Marian, of Katherine's children who didn't appreciate her, of anyone who had loving parents.

Thankfully the village arrived, and Georgette was able to slip off to the teashop to choose a few things for Katherine's family. Katherine enjoyed Georgette's odd teas, and Georgette wanted to do what she could to ease her friend's burden. Georgette made quite a large order when she included buying for herself, for Katherine, and for the poor doctor who was going to be flooded with Lizette's family.

After she made her purchases, they headed towards the new doctor's office. As the three women approached, they found Katherine standing outside. She was upset, and Anna held out her arms. Katherine seemed to sink into them.

"I try not to say anything," Katherine said into Anna's arms. "You've seen. I know you do the same with your children. I try to hold my tongue. John's a full-grown man. He's in his fifties, you know. With a grown son of his own, and yet—I'm still his mother. And…and…oh!"

"That never stops," Anna agreed. "Lizette is a difficult woman."

"Sour! Talking to her is like cuddling a hedgehog with the spikes out. All the time. You can never do anything right. His health isn't great, Anna. He can't hold her hand and stay awake for days which is what I think she wants. You'd think she'd care that he's in pain too. That he's in pain all the time."

Georgette was looking at a woman with a motive, she thought, and she didn't like that at all. She took Marian's hand for comfort. Was this what it was like when you were a parent? Because that agonized confession was painful to hear. Just watching Katherine's frustration and worry was painful. The seething jealousy Georgette had been feeling was rising again and she wanted to clock Lizette. Perhaps another blow would help her realize what she had in a mother-in-law. Katherine was so kind. She'd have loved Lizette if it were possible.

Georgette saw Lucy inside and side-stepped the hugging friends, leaving them to their whispered conversation to check on Lucy instead.

Lucy looked up at the sound of the bell and then rose quickly to cross to Georgette, glancing back behind her as she did. Her gaze was wide and she pressed her finger over her lips. There was a tirade happening in the back room.

"What is happening?" Georgette whispered.

Lucy's voice was barely a breath when she replied. "There's no pleasing that woman. She doesn't feel well. You can see that her head hurts, but more medicine isn't good for her."

"Can't the doctor do anything?" Georgette had to admit she had little faith in his ability.

"Dr. West is trying so hard," Lucy whispered, "but there's no pleasing her. He muttered something about laudanum. I think he only wants to her to be quiet."

"I only now arrived," Georgette whispered dryly, "and I want her to be quiet."

They both leapt when the woman's voice rose in rage.

Georgette tucked Lucy close and whispered, "You don't have to stay, darling."

"I can't leave Dr. West now," Lucy said. "She has stitches on the back of her head and her husband struggles to get around."

"Did she say anything about who hurt her?"

Lucy shook her head. "Mr. Lynd has asked her about a hundred times, but she says she doesn't remember yesterday at all."

Lucy's tone said she didn't believe it, and Georgette didn't either. There was a sound of a crash and Lucy leapt in Georgette's grasp.

"I'll take this one," Georgette said. There was no way she was sending her tender-hearted ward into the room with that villain. She had thought that Lizette would save her venom for her family, but Georgette should have known better.

She crossed to the back room and found the doctor standing outside the door. He wasn't in the view of the inhabitants of the room, and he blushed deeply when he saw Georgette. "I—"

"You're leaving?" Lizette demanded of her husband. Thankfully the couple couldn't see the eavesdroppers.

Georgette met the doctor's gaze. He looked as if he was about to flee out the back and never return to Harper's Hollow.

"Sweetheart," John said. "I have to move or I won't be able to walk tomorrow."

"A person tried to kill me. Probably someone you know, and you're going to abandon me?"

Georgette noted the emphasis, but she didn't think the doctor had. Someone he knew? Who might know where his mother lived and who knew Lizette was going to be in Harper's Hollow when she'd appeared unexpectedly? That didn't quite add up.

"I'm not leaving you," John protested. "I'm just going to walk down the street and back. You aren't alone. My mother is here. Dr. West is here. Lucy is here."

"All useless! Your mother! What can she do?"

"You won't be alone. I'd never leave you alone after you got hurt, Zette baby, you know I love you."

There was a ringing cold laugh and then Lizette snapped, "But you did leave me, didn't you? You left me and then I got hurt. And now you're leaving me again."

"Zette," John groaned. "I have to work. Of course I have to work. Leaving you to earn money for our family isn't abandoning you. I couldn't have known what was going to happen. I'm sure Detective Aaron will find who attacked you soon, and you won't have to be afraid anymore."

"Oh do you think so?" Lizette's tone was cruel. "Why can't you just man through your pain? I am struggling through mine."

"I can't stop being injured, Zette. If I don't move, I'll be in the bed next to you. You know that—"

Her low-pitched muttering had John sitting back down. Georgette had enough. She walked into the room and told John, "Out."

"Excuse me?"

"Out," Georgette ordered. "You know it wasn't me that hurt her, and your wife needs a moment to collect herself. The doctor has strict orders that she settle down and you need to leave for that to happen."

"A moment?" Lizette snapped. "Who do you think you are?"

"Go, Mr. Lynd. I won't leave her until you get back."

Georgette pulled John Lynd from his chair and nudged him towards the door. "Doctor, go with him. You both need fresh air."

8

GEORGETTE DOROTHY AARON

"You are acting like a spoiled child, making the people around you miserable."

Lizette glared at Georgette. "I'm the victim here. I was attacked!"

"If I hadn't found you myself, I'd question whether you were lying." Georgette took John's seat and waited for the bell to ring again. "Why are you playing games with what happened?"

"Games? I'm an injured woman here. Why are you attacking me?"

"You sidestepped answering who hurt you."

The woman's head tilted and she shrugged. "I was confused. I don't know who hurt me. I don't know what happened. I don't remember yesterday." Her gaze was fixed on the wall, arms crossed over her chest, and Georgette found it as believable as a child with pie on her face swearing she hadn't touched the pie.

"I don't believe you."

Lizette Lynd's gaze narrowed on Georgette.

Georgette's narrowed in return on Lizette.

"Who are you protecting? And why would you protect them?"

Lizette shrugged, a stubborn expression on her face.

"If Joseph does find a tramp in Harper's Hollow, you'll be putting the poor man through a lot of trouble. Who was it that hurt you?"

Lizette sniffed, staring at the wall. "I don't know what happened. I don't know who hurt me, but I think it was probably a tramp."

Georgette was convinced that Lizette was lying. It wasn't what the woman was saying, but how she said it. The way she glanced at Georgette out of the side of her eye, the way she had a little smile that came and went. This wasn't a woman who seemed afraid. She wasn't worried about a madman bursting through the door and finishing his work. If anything, she seemed calculating.

If Georgette were honest with herself, there was a large part of her that wished to pick up her own broken fence post and strike the woman down. She shook her head and remained quiet, wondering if silence would help. It didn't. The woman was immovable and refused to say anything but complaints. The amount of dislike rising up in Georgette shocked her, and she bit down on her bottom lip.

"Do you need anything?" she asked, trying to calm her inner rage.

"I'm surprised you care."

"If I didn't care, I wouldn't be here," Georgette snapped, losing patience. "Lucy wouldn't be here, Joseph wouldn't be investigating, people wouldn't be making food for your family and checking in on you."

"They don't care about me. They care about Katherine. She's got everyone fooled. She's not a saint, you know. Everyone acts like she's perfect, but she isn't. She's as human as the rest of us."

Georgette stood and walked to the window, watching John pass by. He hadn't walked to the end of the street as he'd suggested. Instead he hobbled down a few buildings, turned and went back and forth.

"How long have you been married to John?"

Lizette eyed Georgette as though she thought she was being judged, but Georgette only glanced back out the window and Lizette finally answered begrudgingly. "We met when we were young. Very young really. In chorus for a Christmas production. Ever since then, we've loved each other."

Georgette smiled. There was a bit of softness in Lizette when she talked about John at that moment, and it seemed Lizette might not be so bad.

"I was stupid."

Georgette winced, immediately changing her mind.

"I threw all my eggs in the Lynd basket without taking a bigger look at the world. Like I said, I was stupid. He's a dreamer. Always imagining and hoping, but in reality? We're scraping by."

Georgette searched for a reply and then pointed out, "Much of the world is scraping by."

"You aren't," Lizette accused. "You're not digging up carrots in the garden, hoping to find a few more, begging for scraps of cabbage, or more eggs. We have nothing to offer our children except watery cabbage soup. Maybe it would be different if he weren't—what he is."

"What is he?" Georgette asked quietly.

"An injured dreamer who wouldn't work hard even if he could. He was a has-been before he even started."

"He loves you."

"And more the fool me, I love him too. Would that I had been more commercial than romantic when I married. Oh look—he's hobbling this way now. You can always hear him thumping along slow and uneven. He doesn't have the faith to be healed, he doesn't have the wit to not get injured, he doesn't have the will to work through the pain. He doesn't—" Lizette snapped her mouth shut again.

When John appeared in the door, Georgette left the room, squeezing his arm as she passed. Georgette felt certain that Joseph needed to pin down Lizette again. There was no way that woman was telling the truth.

❦

"No wonder Katherine doesn't like her," Georgette announced as she got behind the wheel of the auto. "I was tempted to put her out of her misery, and she isn't even married to my child. I can't imagine. Every Christmas with that dark shadow in the corner. Every child's birthday. Every family dinner. I'd rather be single than facing that voice over the dinner table. Her poor, poor husband."

"There has never been any question that John loves her," Anna told Georgette. "That's part of the problem.

He does love her. He adores her and doesn't seem to see or hear it when she's venomous. And there's a further issue—"

Anna sounded sick and Georgette pulled the auto to the side of the road to face her.

"Lizette is insinuating that Katherine needs to sell her house and help her children—particularly her oldest son. That doing otherwise is selfish."

Georgette stared in shock and Marian choked in the back and then muttered about family voices and the definition of selfishness. Georgette started the auto, her mind skipping through the idea of Katherine selling her house and financing a few more years of her son's life. Georgette shook her head. Money ran out—Georgette knew that all too well. Money ran out, and you were left to struggle with what you had to offer. The best plan wasn't to give the children money. That was like giving fish to a starving man when you could teach him to fish for himself. Sometimes all you needed was the tools.

They acquired the meal Eunice had made and delivered it to Katherine's house.

"Emmanuline, darling," Anna said to the woman who opened the door.

Georgette smiled, holding the pan of food and Emmanuline accepted the over-sized pan. "Come in, come in. You all are so kind."

The woman was younger than her brother by a good number of years, but if Georgette remembered right, Emmanuline was the youngest while John was the oldest. "We've brought your family a few things. Are more coming?"

"Eventually." Emmanuline laughed. "It's hard to...to...

drop everything. Jedediah and his wife have seven children. They can't just get on the train and come sit by Lizette's bed. I'm sure Jed will be here soon, but given how Lizette will be all right, he's not going to take off work early."

"So, only you could come?"

"It's Friday," Emmanuline said with a quiet voice. "They'll all be here. It'll be loud and noisy as Mum always wants, but she won't be here to enjoy it. Not until Lizette comes home, and then she'll probably run Mum ragged taking care of her."

Georgette glanced at Anna and then Marian before saying, "You don't sound like you're a very big fan of your sister."

"Sister-in-law," Emmanuline clarified and Georgette was quite sure that Emmanuline had come to help her mother and brother and not the injured party. "How are you, Anna?"

Georgette gestured to Marian and they helped unload the boxes and baskets of things they'd brought for the family. As Katherine lived alone and spent much of her time outside of her house, usually doing good work, there was no way she was prepared to have her children and grandchildren appear unexpectedly and feed them.

Once they had everything inside the house, they piled back into the auto.

"I think we've learned a very specific lesson today," Georgette said as she drove back home.

"What's that?" Anna asked.

"To be grateful for the families we have," Georgette muttered. "I need to get home and cleanse my palette from being around poor Katherine's family."

Anna laughed. "It's not quite as it seems, you know. Emmanuline is a good daughter and they spend a lot of time together. Her children adore Katherine, and Jedediah is the same. He doesn't let Lizette's sourness extend to his days. He protects his mother as he can. Katherine doesn't let them protect her fully. If she did, she'd lose time with John, and she'd rather deal with Lizette than lose out on John entirely."

Georgette parked the auto outside of her house and let the dogs out. Anna returned to her house and Marian went inside, but rather than go in with the sourness that was growing in her own heart, Georgette took the dogs to the back garden and threw sticks for them. She was out there until Charles came to find her.

"Are you all right?" he asked, taking the stick from her and throwing it for the dogs and then tugging her close.

Georgette's mouth screwed up in an attempt not to weep. "I miss my mother."

Charles's face was shocked. "I—"

"It's all right, darling," she said, wrapping her arms around Charles. "I just—I—it's hard to explain."

He crossed to the stone bench and pulled her down beside him. "You're rather good with words, you know."

Georgette laughed and was surprised to find it was a watery sound. That made her laugh harder, and there was no question that she seemed at least half-mad. She laid her head on his shoulder and apologized.

"Are you all right?"

"I'm jealous and I don't like it. I'm sad and I think that's only the baby messing with my mind and heart. I'm worried about Katherine and I despise her daughter-in-law, but I know Katherine looks for the good in people. I want to rage at the world, but I'm not actually sure why, and I want to shake both Joseph and Marian until their teeth clack in their head."

Charles tangled their fingers together. "Well, I don't know what to do with any of that."

"Your being here helps. Did you get work done?"

His brows lifted and he admitted, "I did actually. Rather a lot of it, to be honest. I think Luther will be pleased since I did a few of the less desirable things. He's turned out to rather like this arrangement of me working here once or twice a week."

"That's good," Georgette told him. She'd have been worried if he was worried, but since he wasn't, she wasn't going to bother with it.

He lifted her fingers and kissed each one. "We've got to go get our Janey."

"Yes," she said, instantly feeling brighter. "Janey, Snow White and the Seven Dwarves, a delightful step into the pub. I'm looking forward to stew and a few sips from your pint."

$$\text{❈}\quad 9 \quad\text{❈}$$

CHARLES AARON

Georgette needed to write. He suspected that if she could sink into a story, she'd feel better. She'd been prone to tears over the last few months, but it was worse in the last week or two. It was as if she couldn't quite get any of her stories right in her head or on the page, and everything else was darker because of that change. He also thought she might need some time alone, but he wasn't loving the idea.

The publisher in him needed his star author to write because he had stories to sell. Publishing in an economic depression was a risky business. Having an excellent author people loved, working hard? That made it easier. Georgette didn't pretend to write fiction for the ages, but she did have a wicked insight into mankind when she could flex it. It was unfortunate that the same insight that let her write excellent novels also left her able to guess at the motivations of people and why they might commit crimes. If only she would stop helping deliver dinners or taking on the little ones as she had.

When adding not having a story going well to her other concerns, she was suffering. He reminded himself again that her parents had been gone for more than a decade and that Eunice was a stoic, silent type. Being his wife, having people notice her, having to interact with the children, it was a lot for a woman who had been overlooked and alone for far too long.

They'd decided to not tell their neighbors that Georgette was "Joseph Jones" and it was the best plan they'd come up with yet. Some of them realized she wrote, but none of them realized she was the famous author. It turned out that Georgette, who'd been starving for human interaction, was now being smothered by it. His Georgie was the type of person who needed humans in very limited ways.

Janey's school was near Ely, as was the theater. They drove in silence, but he thought Georgette needed the quiet. She was probably thinking about that Lynd woman who'd been hit over the head. Charles's own mind moved to the woman and away again. He had no doubt as to where Marian's thoughts went.

The movie was a delight and he hoped it lifted Georgette's spirits. He doubted Marian was comforted by the happily-ever-after given the state of her own. Janey was over the moon and talked about it as they drove toward the pub for dinner.

Georgette's gaze flicked to a nearby orphan home and he sighed. "Go ahead. Janey and I will meet you at the pub."

Georgette got out of the auto, and Marian gasped and followed.

"How do you think they draw those movies?" Janey asked, chattering. "Why do you think Georgette is going there?" A thought struck Janey and she asked in a trembling voice, "Are you going to move me?"

Charles shook his head instantly. "No, no."

He briefly recapped what had happened to Lizette Lynd and then told Janey that until they discovered the perpetrator, she needed to stay in the garden or the house. She'd been so well-raised by her parents that she nodded without question.

"Is Georgette all right?" Janey asked.

"She's all right," Charles answered, hoping he wasn't lying.

It only took Georgette and Marian a few minutes to arrive at the pub.

"Unsurprisingly," she told Charles, "Katherine was there during the time when Lizette Lynd was hurt."

"That's what we thought, right?" Marian asked.

"Right," Georgette and Charles replied in unison.

JOSEPH AARON

Joseph watched as Charles seated his wife into the auto, along with Marian in the back seat. The dogs were whining at Joseph's feet, and he reached down to pet them all, giving Henry special attention. He was rather afraid that the days of thinking Henry was his dog would soon be over.

He turned and found Eunice watching him watch them.

"Would you like dinner?"

Joseph sat with Eunice in the kitchen. "Have you met Lizette Lynd?" he asked.

"Just Katherine and once her daughter."

"What do you think happened?"

"Sounds like she's a sourpuss," Eunice said dryly. "For whatever reason she's not talking, why do sourpusses get knocked on the back of the head? Because someone reached their limit and had enough."

"Her husband and mother-in-law have alibis," Joseph told her. "Who else would do it?"

"Think of the people in your life you'd like to knock sideways," Eunice advised, putting a large slice of meat pie on his plate. It was followed by roasted potatoes, carrots, and parsnips. "Would they be your mother or your brother? I'm guessing those are the people you wouldn't hurt."

Joseph laughed darkly and Eunice replied with a corresponding dark grin. "So you wouldn't necessarily knock Charles or Georgette sideways? There are some people on your mind." She grinned wickedly as she added, "I've my own list running for a while."

Joseph shook his head and then admitted, "Never Georgette, possibly Charles." Joseph laughed. "I'd consider a few other more peripheral people in my life."

"While you're considering that," Eunice said, "consider that Lizette's periphery people have seen her twist and torment those they love. I'm a periphery person to you, but if I were bothering Charles—well, you'd want it to stop."

"I've thought of all that," Joseph muttered. "It's not like I'm completely stupid. It's that everyone is either accounted for or entirely unaccounted for. This brother, Jedediah, he was at work. His wife, however, was home with the children. When the local constable asked the little ones if their mother was home the entire day—without leaving—they looked at him as if he'd grown a second head and said nothing. It doesn't mean that his wife was the one who knocked Lizette for a loop, but it means her alibi is uncertain at best. It the same for all the housewives. They all could have done it really. Except perhaps for the fisherman brother who's too far way to have done it."

"Is it like that for all of the ladies?"

"Worse still. Lizette's family is in the general area. No one was seen coming into town, but that doesn't mean anything. They could have avoided scrutiny. We didn't have any reason to have an eye out."

"Country roads could let you get to Katherine's house without being seen." Eunice sighed. "You know, you won't have to wait long. That Lizette is going to be taken home soon. Probably this weekend. Much of the family will come to Katherine's and rally round so-to-speak. You've got disguised lieutenants who could get in and stir the pot."

Joseph groaned. "My supervisor never appreciates the reports that include Georgette, Charles, and Marian. I feel like I'm getting black marks and a letter home to my parents every time I turn one in. I suppose Marian's family might well get what they want and find that they won't have a Yard man for a son-in-law."

Eunice didn't reply to that, but her eyes were full of

something. A greater wisdom brought by experience. For all that she'd been single her entire life and an adjunct to Georgette's family, Eunice seemed to have a wealth of knowledge about relationships, marriages, and family. Her entire philosophy boiled down to saying nothing, but there were worlds of opinions behind those eyes.

Joseph finished his meal and then crossed through the back garden to the path that led to Katherine's house. He kept watch for any sign of someone who had made a makeshift camp, as transients were wont to do. Any time he came upon a clearing with the possibility or even a thinning in the trees, Joseph explored and came up with the certainty that the children he hoped to have someday would love this wood. And that there was no reason to believe that anyone was camping in the wood nefariously.

He groaned and then hurried along the path, no longer bothering to explore. Barnaby Mustly spent far more time in the wood than Joseph did, and Barnaby seemed convinced that there wasn't anyone around who shouldn't be. Joseph would go out with Barnaby the next day just to be sure. Maybe there would be evidence that meant nothing to Barnaby but might have meaning for Joseph. He doubted it, however, but he needed to be thorough.

As he approached the back of Katherine's house, he noted the children running in the orchard, laughing. Two men were standing at the back of the house, talking to each other, eyes on the children, but their tone and attitude was secretive.

Joseph decided to approach from the side. If he sneaked up on them their reaction could be telling. He walked around the edge of the orchard. The two sons seemed unrelated except they were in the exact same stance. Both had their arms crossed over their chests, one leg relaxed, and they both had rounded out in the stomachs, but one was quite a bit taller. The other was smaller and narrower. Both were much slimmer than John Lynd, who had moved from a rounded stomach to a full butter ball.

Once he got closer, Joseph saw that they looked more similar than he expected. They had the same jaw, the same dark brown eyes, the same look on their faces when they realized Joseph had appeared.

"Who are you?" demanded the larger Lynd son.

"Detective Inspector Joseph Aaron."

Joseph held out his hand and shook both of theirs, lifting his brows until he got their names. The larger one was Jedediah and the smaller one was Mitchell. Both eyed Joseph as if he was entirely unwanted. It was, he thought, an interesting reaction. He wouldn't have expected them to shut down. He'd have expected them to demand answers.

One of the children ran into the wood and neither of the Lynd men even look bothered.

The men exchanged looks and the smaller one said, "Here about Lizette, I suppose."

"I am. She doesn't seem to have any information to help me or direct the case. Do you have anything?"

Both shook their heads without looking at each other, but they also used that moment to let their gazes drift to the children as if they were checking on them. Joseph didn't believe that for a second. He didn't believe any of this.

"You know who it is, don't you?"

The brothers exchanged glances once again before focusing on Joseph. Mitchell shook his head, but neither of them answered.

"Is Katherine here?"

"Our mother is still at the doctor's office. They're going to bring Lizette and John back here. Lizette says she needs to recover longer before she can go home, but the doctor decided that she was healthy enough to make the trip and didn't need to be attended constantly."

Jedediah muttered under his breath, but neither of them expanded.

"She seems like a difficult woman," Joseph tried.

Neither of them answered.

"It's odd that she doesn't remember why she was here. Do either of you know why she might have come when Katherine wasn't here?"

Again, neither of them answered.

Joseph held back his frustration as he asked, "What about your mother?"

"What about her?" The contained frustration in Mitchell's voice had Joseph holding back a smile.

"What about her?" Joseph asked. "The accident happened at her house, Lizette is a difficult woman, it seems likely that your mother would have a good reason to want to silence a daughter-in-law like that and save her son from a hard marriage. Maybe your mother had enough?"

"She would never!" Jedediah shouted. The children went immediately silent. "My mother isn't here," he growled. "We weren't here during the accident and none of us know anything. You need to leave."

❧ 10 ❧

CHARLES AARON

"Wake up," he whispered. "Wake up."

His finger was already pressed against his wife's lips and when her eyes squinted against the lamplight, he tugged her upright. The way she blinked in groggy surprise was adorable.

Charles had already dressed in a casual suit, though the sun was still down, and he had her dress, coat, and hat ready. He whisper-ordered her through dressing.

While she escaped to the bath to wash her face and teeth and take care of her other business, Charles disappeared to finish his preparations. By the time Georgette had buttoned herself into her clothes, he had returned and waved her after him, finger still over his lip.

They tip-toed to the back garden, where Charles had already gathered breakfast buns, fruit, cheese, and a thermos of tea. He handed Georgette a steaming mug, made how she liked and then tugged her out the door. The dogs tripped behind them as though they knew that he was arranging an adventure, and there wasn't a peep out of them other than the click of their nails against the floors.

Charles seated her in the auto and then joined her after putting the dogs in the back.

"Charles?" Georgette was slowly waking with the help of the tea.

"We're having an adventure."

"An adventure?"

"Darling Georgie, have you not noticed we've been invaded?"

She smiled at him and despite her morning sickness, which he knew she suffered daily, she seemed happy. Perhaps because she was holding that large mug of tea. It was the kind with cocoa and coffee along with black tea, and she adored it more than almost anything else.

Charles started the auto and pulled onto the road.

"What are we doing?" Georgette asked. She'd found the blanket he'd put in the auto, wrapped it around herself, and snuggled against his arm.

"We're escaping."

"Our own house?"

He laughed as he repeated, "We've been invaded. We need time away."

Georgette nodded against his shoulder and sighed deeply. It took mere moments for her to relax. He motored through the countryside, looking at his notes. When he'd mentioned to Joseph that he was sneaking Georgette out, Joseph had suggested that they see if it were possible to take the back roads between the houses where two of the Lynd siblings had purchased homes together. The sun had risen as they drove and the morning was lovely in shades of oranges and pinks.

He drove slowly, in no hurry to return home, and watched for someone who might have noticed the passing of an auto on a generally untraveled road. "You know what I think is interesting?"

Georgette shook her head against his shoulder. She glanced up at him, and then at the tea mug. Finally, she sat up and started to refill her mug, carefully balancing against the slow rumble of the auto.

"That the Lynds chose to live near each other. We seem to be doing the same. I told Robert about your idea that we'd find him a house and see if we could update it over time, and he was intrigued. He said he'd never want to live in Harper's Hollow without us there, but he'd never want to live anywhere else if we were in Harper's Hollow."

Georgette wove her fingers through Charles's and let him have a sip of her tea. "That makes me happy."

"My nephews adore you. And they love having a place for holidays. Robert told me it was as though he had a childhood home again."

"Oh, I like that," she replied. She snuggled back into his side. "What do you think we should look for?"

"He's not in a hurry," Charles reminded her. "Like Joseph, he has some of the money from their parents' home sale. He's added to it, so he isn't starting with nothing."

Georgette paused and then asked Charles what was on her mind. "What about Joseph and Marian?"

He stiffened under her shoulder and she stiffened

along with him. "I'm afraid that there isn't anything that we can do. If we interfere, they might just turn on us."

"Would that they'd turn on her parents," Georgette muttered. "Let's not worry about that."

They stopped to enjoy the breakfast he'd brought as the dogs sniffed the area.

"What do you think of the name Charles for a son?" Georgette asked.

"No," Charles said instantly. "No. Of course not. What about George?"

Georgette laughed. "No. That makes my skin crawl. What about your brother's name?"

"Philip? No, if someone is going to name a child after him, it should be Robert or Joseph."

"What about Hazel for a girl? Octavia?"

"I like Octavia," Charles replied, kissing her fingers. "What about a literature name? We did fall in love over books, didn't we?"

Georgette hummed her agreement and then took another sip of tea. "I like books. And you. And falling in love over books. Perhaps name from a Jane Austen."

"Wentworth," Charles shot out instantly. "I am half-agony, half-hope."

"Oh yes!" Georgette said and then pointed at a little cottage right near the door. "Anne or Wentworth. Unless we decided to be quite normal and choose Frederick."

They finished the meal and drove along the road once more until they reached a cottage set close enough to have a good view of the passing automobiles.

Charles stopped the auto near the cottage.

Georgette eyed him suspiciously and then laughed. "Is this the adventurous part? Questioning the locals?"

He grinned. "Two birds with one stone."

The two of them approached the door and Charles knocked. At first, there was no answer.

"Hello," Georgette called. "Hello there?"

A woman in an apron came to the door and Georgette smiled engagingly. "Hullo there."

"Hello," the woman said, wiping the flour from her hands with her apron. "If you've got trouble with your automobile, I don't have a telephone."

"We were actually wondering if you could answer questions for us. This road seems very quiet."

"It is," she said. "No one takes this road when the other is so much faster. It's a direct route to anywhere people want to go. Mostly only ramblers go through here and not so much now. Those tend to be students."

"What about tramps?"

"You never know when some poor homeless fellow is going to come walking through," she said. "But it's not so often."

"What about last Thursday? Did someone drive through here?"

The woman started to shake her head and then she paused. "You know, there was a black auto that drove by."

"Did you see who was driving?"

"Just heard it. I looked out and saw the tail end of it. It could have been anyone driving the auto. Heck, it could have been a ghost behind the wheel. I'd never have known the difference."

"But there was an auto?" Charles asked. "Do you think you'd recognize it if you saw it again?"

She shook her head. "Why are you asking?"

"We're trying to track someone's movements. There was a bit of an accident."

"Is the person all right?"

Charles smiled his professional smile and nodded. "Everyone's going to be just fine. I suppose we're partially out here just to have a quiet ride together as well as test our theory." His charming grin quieted whatever concern the woman had.

He knew Georgette was considering the woman in that way she had. The woman had come quickly to the window and answered readily. Charles could well imagine she peeked often on who was going where. Most of the drivers that passed her home might well be people she knew. Outside of the wireless, what could be more intriguing?

"Well, I don't know what it would matter," the woman said. "Driving down here or not. Nothing to see. Most folks don't come this way. That's all I can tell you for sure."

"We appreciate it," Georgette said, a happy grin on her face that Charles knew was from experience instead of true feeling. "You were ever so helpful."

They left a few moments later and Georgette said to Charles, "We should stop by Katherine's house using this route and see if any of them have black sedans."

"We should," he agreed. "Though perhaps with Joseph along as well."

"We could stop in town to bring them a treat. Some friendly excuse to barge into their family and verify rising tensions."

Charles laughed and they finished their drive, passing Katherine's house just as tea was approaching. Outside of the house, three autos stood at the ready, two black sedans and a farmer's truck. Charles looked at his wife who met his gaze and nodded. Things had already been pointing at one of the family being the one who'd struck down Lizette Lynd. Who else would know that Lizette would be there? Who else would be able to follow her? Who would have a grudge?

It seemed that the criminal had to be someone who knew just what Lizette was and perhaps more—just how her venom affected those around her.

☙❧

MARIAN PARKER

Marian woke at the creak on the stairs, and she peeked out the door. There was a part of her who wanted the person on the stairs to be Joseph, demanding that they discuss what had gone wrong between them, but it wasn't. Charles had a small smile on his face as he led the half-asleep Georgette down the stairs. He saw Marian over Georgette's shoulder and winked, putting a finger to his lips as Georgette yawned deeply.

She nodded and forced a smile and then shut the door to her room. She knew that if she returned to bed, she wouldn't sleep, so she took a sheet of paper, a lap writing desk, and pen and returned to her bed.

On one side of the sheet, she wrote "Pros of Marrying Joseph." On the flip side of the sheet, she wrote "Cons of Marrying Joseph." She fiddled with her pen as she stared at the cons list and then slowly wrote out: I'll disappoint my parents. I'll be alone often. His work is dangerous, and I may be widowed early.

She wrote stupid things that didn't really matter to her next: He snuffles when he falls asleep on the train. He's angry with my parents.

After a long moment of introspection, she added: rightfully.

Marian wanted to be angry with him, but she wasn't entirely blind. Her father and mother had been slowly and conscientiously trying to put a wedge between her and Joseph. What surprised her was that they seemed to care so very much.

Perhaps Mother, who had often been alone with the children while Father worked, had a point. Who knew better than Mother the effect of having a husband long at work while you were home with the children? But Marian guessed that many women experienced such things. Why Joseph? Why was he so objectionable?

Marian knew that they didn't love how his entire family —until recently—had been a trio of bachelors. But they weren't anymore. Robert was a bit young to marry, but Joseph was ready to settle down. And Charles had waited far too long, to the great fortune of both him and Georgette.

Perhaps her parents worried that Joseph wouldn't appreciate her because his family was so fractured? Marian was certain that the opposite was true. All three of the Aaron men worshipped Georgette because she had returned the sense of family to their lives.

Marian got out of bed and paced her bedroom. If she threw Joseph over, she knew he'd be upset. She believed he loved her, and she knew she loved him. He'd heal, however, and then he'd look for another wife. One who would put him first.

Her stomach dropped, sickened. There were no pros on the side of the list to marry Joseph, but the most important one didn't need to be written. If she didn't marry him, she'd regret it for the rest of her life. She'd spend every passing year wondering what her life would have been like with Joseph. Even if she fell in love and married another, every fight, every hard time, Marian would wonder how it would have been with Joseph. Because, she thought, she'd never stop loving him.

Why then was she being so stupid and letting her parents succeed in getting their wedge into place?

❧ 11 ❧

JOSEPH AARON

"Worthless!" Constable Higgins sat behind his desk, looking at the pile of their notes. "And a huge waste of time."

They'd spent the last few hours going over every single piece of evidence. Every single thing they'd learned. "I'll be damned if it wasn't one of those Lynds that clocked the woman. If she's not going to report who it was, I say we title it family squabble and move on with our work."

Joseph nodded. What else could they do? Lizette Lynd didn't want their help. The Lynd family either knew it was one of them or suspected it, and they'd closed ranks. If no one else in the town was in danger, why drag out the investigation?

The bell to the police office rang and both men looked up to find Charles.

"Where is Georgette?"

"Sleeping in the auto." He glanced back and then said, "We found the route and we verified an auto did take that road. But it was a black sedan—it'll never help a court case, even I know that."

"Do the Lynds have a black sedan?"

"They have two that I saw," Charles said. "We talked to a woman who said that she'd seen the black auto but she refused to say if she could recognize it again. It is possible to take a route between where the Lynds live and where Katherine lives without needing to use a road into the village. That might even be their preference," he added. "The route was delightful to be honest." Charles rubbed the back of his neck and then shook his head. "It doesn't do you any good, does it? Georgette told me that Lizette is refusing to speak."

"They all are," Joseph said. "Higgins and I had just decided that we're going to chalk it up to a family dispute. No one has died, they clearly don't want our help, all evidence points to it being a family person and not a rampaging tramp. We're done here. I'll write my report Monday morning and go back to Scotland Yard."

"Fabulous," Charles said dryly. "Family dinner tomorrow night. Robert is coming in. Georgette has some mad plan for him that he's indulging."

Joseph lifted his brows and pasted a smile on his face, but he hadn't really heard his uncle. Or he'd heard it, but he didn't care all that much. Instead he nodded and rose.

"I'm going for a walk." He nodded to the constable and said, "Next time, my friend, we're just having fish and chips and a football game. No more intransigent woman who doesn't want our help."

Joseph walked out of the police station and glanced

both ways before deciding upon the walk next to the river. He would follow it and find his head, he hoped.

GEORGETTE DOROTHY AARON

Georgette got out of the auto with her dogs when she saw Katherine Lynd and told Charles with a wink, "I'll see you at home."

Katherine was out and out moseying. Georgette watched her for a moment as she walked down the road. The woman leaned over and sniffed some of the late-blooming flowers. She slowly stood upright again and then said something to one of the children passing by. The little one grinned widely and hugged Katherine's leg before being tugged away by her mother.

Katherine was, without question, the kindest woman that Georgette had ever seen. Georgette crossed to her, catching up as she paused once again.

"You don't want to go home."

Katherine started and then turned on Georgette. Tears filled Katherine's eyes and her bottom lip trembled. "I hate having her in my house."

"I don't blame you," Georgette said, tucking her arm through Katherine's. "What if we were to go have a good pot of tea and too many cakes?"

Katherine nodded and they walked to the teashop together, taking the table in the corner. Georgette didn't ask any questions and Katherine didn't volunteer any information, but a tear or two slipped down her face while Georgette plied her with tea and cakes. It was the silence that Katherine needed and when they finished their tea, Georgette walked her home. Katherine took a fortifying breath.

Before she left, Georgette reminded her, "This is your house."

"Lizette sees it as hers. Eldest son and all that."

"Disabuse her of the notion."

Katherine bit down on her bottom lip and then met Georgette's gaze. "One of my children hurt Lizette. They know who did it, but I don't. The problem is that Lizette thinks she has this...this...ability to use that information over all of them."

Georgette had seen people get away with their crimes before. She didn't see why this moment needed to be any different. She knew it was callous. She knew it made Lizette nothing more than a one-layered villain who deserved what had happened to her.

But the thing was—Katherine. It was Katherine for Georgette. Katherine was being tortured by her daughter-in-law when Georgette would be grateful every day for having such a woman willing to look at her as family, treat her as family, love her as family. Lizette was such dimwit that Georgette didn't care if she suffered a little for whatever she was trying to do to Katherine and her children.

Georgette took a long look at Katherine and repeated, "This is your house. This is your house, your family, you're in charge. As long as your children are united and you with them, I'm not sure she can be all that effective against you."

Katherine stared at Georgette. "That's some Machiavellian hijinks."

Georgette laughed. "You—I—you're a surprise, Katherine."

Katherine chased Georgette's comment with a little girl's giggle. "I wasn't always a grandmother. I've read. I've lived more than just in an orchard near the wood in tiny little village. This is me now, Georgette. Not me always."

Georgette laughed again and then glanced beyond Katherine where her grandchildren were playing under those trees. "You're right. This isn't me always either. Not so long ago, I was the town's old maid who was slowly losing more and more money and without prospects. Eunice and I would have died slowly of starvation or ended in a debtor's prison. Do they still have those?"

Katherine looked up in surprise. "No, they don't. You might have starved or gotten weak and then sick. It's hard to get over an illness when we're already dying."

"I know I'm lucky."

"You're lucky." Katherine hugged Georgette. "Because you are loved."

"I'm not the only one who is lucky. Your children love you. Protect them back, darling."

Katherine nodded and Georgette left her, making her way back to her house through the wood. She had run until it hurt the other day. This time the walk was idyllic. She wasn't worried anymore. It was nice to feel safe where you lived. That thought was chased by the thought of Lizette.

Georgette had suggested to Katherine that they should stand against the woman. The rising feeling of guilt was not one that Georgette enjoyed. She stretched her neck as she considered what she'd said. She should be kinder than that, Georgette thought. Lizette might be negative and she might be playing games with her family, but surely any woman deserved to feel safe in her own home, among her own family?

Georgette paused when she heard a rustle in the trees and she clucked to her dogs, ordering in a whisper, "Quiet."

There was a snap of a branch and Georgette's heart leapt. She stepped back, bending to grab Susan's collar. Susan, of all Georgette's dogs, was the liveliest. Another branch snapped and Georgette grasped Susan's mouth, holding her jaw shut, but the dog's tail was wagging frantically.

A low curse followed, and Georgette stood. "Joseph?"

He stepped forward. "I thought I saw something."

Susan tugged away and darted for Joseph, and Georgette followed. He held a piece of paper clenched in his hand, but it was his face that had Georgette concerned.

"Are you all right?"

His answer was a dark curse.

"Joseph!" Georgette reached out and touched his wrist lightly. "Are you all right?"

"No." He shoved the paper at Georgette and then repeated. "No. Not at all."

He pushed past Georgette and headed to his cottage. Georgette considered following to make sure he made it home, but she knew he didn't want her around. If he'd wanted her, he'd have stayed. He'd have walked her home. He'd have told her the problem.

Slowly Georgette uncrumpled the paper and read. Her stomach dropped as she did. It read:

Cons of Marrying Joseph

I'll disappoint my parents.
I'll be alone often.
His work is dangerous, and I may be widowed early.
He snuffles when he falls asleep on the train.
He's angry with my parents. Rightfully.

Georgette winced. Her mind was making a division that made her highly uncomfortable. Marian was Georgette's first true friend. That couldn't change. She considered the pain that would be caused if Marian and Joseph fell apart. He lived in the village and spent nearly every meal with Georgette and Charles. She pressed her finger between her eyebrows against the rising headache.

Joseph was important to Georgette, and he was her family. That wouldn't ever change. Charles, Joseph, and Robert were a unit who had accepted Georgette and given her a place to belong. They all shared the same name. They would share the same holidays. Regardless of Marian, their children would live and grow together. They were choosing each other every day.

Georgette leaned against a tree as she realized that Marian would have another family if she left Joseph. She would have a husband and children that belonged to another and along with that—whoever that man was—he wouldn't want Marian in the pocket of the Aaron family. No man would want their wife spending her days among the family of a man she had once loved.

Georgette rubbed the back of her neck as the calculation came to an end, and she realized that there was only one way this would end. With Marian and Georgette not as close as before. They wouldn't stop being friends, but Georgette wouldn't be able to walk out her back garden and down the path to Marian's house. The Christmas celebrations the two had planned would never happen. The days of raising their children together would never come.

Marian was necessary to Georgette in a way that made her feel...human. For so long she'd been a ghost. Georgette knew this wasn't about her, though. She needed to process all of this...this...selfishness and decide how to react.

Georgette let the tears fall, waited until the heat left her face and then read the list again.

Cons of Marrying Joseph
I'll disappoint my parents.
I'll be alone often.
His work is dangerous, and I may be widowed early.
He snuffles when he falls asleep on the train.
He's angry with my parents. Rightfully.

She turned over the page and saw the other title. The Pros of Marrying Joseph. The fact that nothing was written there? Georgette read the list again and again. Then she noticed the rightfully. You know, Georgette thought, Marian had never once quibbled when the two friends were together that she did love Joseph. Not once.

Had she been lying? Georgette imagined those days, thought back to them and then she shook her head. There was no way that Marian had been lying. She did love Joseph. And if she did—what if this list wasn't complete? What if Marian was just working things out in her head? If she was trying to process dealing with her parents, Marian needed to know that Joseph had seen and been hurt by the list she had written.

Georgette knew the power of words like these, and she hated seeing them apply in Marian's life in the opposite way of how they'd applied in Georgette's. Georgette still remembered the simple list Charles had written. She'd memorized it, considered it, and it had been enough to assuage her fears and help her to marry him. Her list had read:

-Convince Georgette I love her.
-Convince Georgette to marry me.
-Convince Georgette to find a house for us.
-Find a house with:
-an office so I can work from home at least half the time
-an office for Georgette so she can write dozens more books
-room for children
-room for too many books and more to come
-a garden for smoking pipes in
-a village that has an excellent pub
-create a happily ever after?
-convince Georgette to share her troubles
-convince Georgette to find a village that will work for Joseph and Marian as well

Georgette closed her eyes, having accepted different possible futures and knew the one she would fight for, and then she hurried down the path and towards her home all the while swearing to herself that if it wasn't too late to meddle, she was going to meddle hard, fast, and repeatedly.

❧ 12 ☙

JOSEPH AARON

He wasn't going to think about it. He wasn't going to deal with it. He was going to tell the Lynds they were done and then he was going to go back to London. He didn't have rooms there anymore, but that was what family was for. Robert had rooms and Joseph had a key.

Joseph drove to the Lynd house. By the time he'd exited the vehicle both of the Lynd brothers were standing just outside the door. Arms crossed over chests, eyes in challenge. Joseph didn't bother to smile.

"The case is closed."

"What did you decide?" Mitchell tilted his head. "Did you find a tramp?"

The question infuriated him. He had no doubt that the assaulter came from within the Lynd family and they knew it. Would they have let another poor fellow take the punishment for what they had done?

Joseph glanced between the brothers and was instantly sure that Mitchell was the older one. He thought that Mitchell might have taken over the role from his brother John despite the other being eldest.

"No," Joseph said bluntly. "You all know who did it. You've decided to work together. Lizette has ruined her credibility. At this point, it's a family matter. Try to leave the officials out of your next round of squabbles and avoid knocking someone bloody."

Neither of the brothers replied. There was a round of shouting from the inside and they met Joseph's gaze, snapping their mouths shut.

"Do I need to go in there?"

"The ladies have been hurling insults. No need to worry. A Lynd woman is a high-strung woman. A little noise is our normal." The smooth, lying smile that Mitchell gave Joseph was irritating to them both.

Joseph shook his head, not pretending to believe them. He looked at the house, caught sight of Katherine, felt better about leaving, and then paused to examine both of the black sedans.

"You were seen," he said.

He didn't elaborate and they didn't reply. He returned to his auto, purchased for its size to be a family auto, and scowled deeply.

"Family—" Joseph cursed and left.

Robert's home didn't have a place to keep Joseph's auto, and he usually left it in the village and took the train to London. With another curse, he drove to his cottage. When he stopped the auto, Charles and Robert stepped out of his house. They both had their arms crossed over their chests, unintentionally mirroring the Lynd brothers. It was guaranteed to make Joseph's face hurt.

"Why are you here?"

"Georgette said you were upset."

"Did she tell you why?"

"She said you read something that bothered you, and she doesn't think you have the full picture."

The only reply appropriate was another dark curse.

Robert whistled low and then said, "So we brought Charles's whiskey, Eunice's chocolate cake, and a bag full of fish and chips."

Joseph bit back the urge to curse again as it was becoming a bad habit, but when all his uncle and brother did was step back and lead the way inside, he followed. He lit a cigarette as he passed the door to his house and a moment later, Charles pressed an already poured glass of whiskey into his hand.

Family wasn't so bad, Joseph thought, when they turned on the wireless and leaned back to smoke and drink with you in the silence.

After an hour or two, Joseph growled, "Georgette. She can't know what Marian is really thinking."

Charles chuckled, which annoyed Joseph.

"No one can know what a woman is thinking. They're all an impassable, untranslatable abyss that leaves you feeling stupid."

"Georgette doesn't seem like that," Robert said.

"Georgette writes her current thoughts and worries into her books," Charles said. "If you pay attention, she gives you glimpses."

"Glimpses?" Robert muttered. "If that's what you can get from Georgette—Joseph and I have no hope."

Joseph smothered his reaction with a long drink from his glass. Hope? What was that? He sucked in a long drag from his cigarette. Life was better before he was in love. Loving Marian had added sunshine to his life, it was true, until her parents had stopped swallowing their objections. What was so wrong about him, Joseph didn't know.

Charles didn't leave until well after sundown. And Robert didn't leave at all. When he woke the next morning, Robert was sitting at the table, drinking coffee. He'd made bacon and eggs and when Joseph walked into the kitchen, Robert tossed his brother a bottle of aspirin and gestured to the greasy meal.

GEORGETTE DOROTHY AARON

The next morning before they dressed for church, Georgette asked Marian without a preamble, "Is there something wrong with being happy?"

Marian looked up from the window seat.

"Is there some reason you're torturing the man you love because of the whims of your parents in turning against him?"

"I—"

Georgette, however, wasn't finished. "I love you, Marian. I want you to be happy. I can't understand why you don't seem to want that as well."

"I do," Marian argued. "But I also want a relationship with my parents."

Georgette bit back a screech of rage. Not at Marian, but that the idea that parents could have a wonderful daughter with a good man who loved her and was trying to do right by her and still ruin that for her.

"Joseph saw your list."

Marian gasped.

"He looked fairly broken."

"It wasn't complete. I was only trying to sort out all the voices in my head. That isn't what I think or feel." Marian's voice trembled and her hands were shaking. "Georgette—I've ruined everything."

Georgette shook her head and reached out to take Marian's hands. "Have you hurt him?" Georgette nodded. "Of course you have. But have you ruined everything? I don't think so. I suspect that what you need is a heart-to-heart. We're having a family dinner. Take him for a walk after. Tell him everything. All of your worries and what he means to you. But Marian—"

She looked up, hands still shaking.

"Marrying someone is promising to love, honor, and cherish the man you make your vows to. Those vows don't include the quibble that you only choose the man if your parents agree. You would be making your own family with Joseph. One where your parents aren't welcome in the bed, the bank account, or the career choices."

Marian gasped again because it had been too crass to mention the bed, but Georgette had promised she would do all the meddling that could be meddled.

"Come now," Georgette ordered. "Church first, then a family dinner. Let's dress and then go help Eunice."

It was possible, the goddess Atë thought, that Lizette Lynd could replace Georgette in her affections. Only, of course, for a short time. Lizette Lynd was building a self-caused destruction and she didn't have the talent and wit that made Georgette so appealing to the goddess. Lizette Lynd was, however, quite a temporary enjoyment, mischievous in the nasty delusional way that could destroy the entire Lynd family.

Seeing Georgette and Lizette together appealed in a way that Atë cackled over.

"Mrs. Lynd," Georgette said to Lizette, looking beyond her to where Katherine was leaning on Emmanuline's arm. The brothers, their wives, and the children had already ranged ahead after the church service, except for John Lynd who was trailing quite a ways behind. "What a lovely Sunday. Katherine. Emmanuline," she added as the two caught up.

"I find it's lovely to go to the house of God and reflect upon our behavior," Lizette said grandly. "Our rash and cruel actions."

Georgette lifted her brows. "I find that forgiveness most easily comes when I am forgiving."

Georgette was leaning on Charles's arm and he stifled a laugh, but she could tell he was chuckling behind his mask.

"Are you a righteous woman, Mrs. Aaron?" Lizette Lynd demanded.

"I have much room to grow," Georgette replied flatly. "And you? What is your state of grace?"

"I am afflicted on all sides. Surrounded by cruelty and avarice. No doubt my soul will be much improved for my suffering."

Both Katherine and Emmanuline had paled. The old Georgette would have snapped her mouth closed and made an inane comment. The new Georgette—or the one who had finally found her voice—said, "A suffering that you distribute to those around you. I hope that you never come to the end of their mercy and tolerance."

Charles tugged Georgette away, still trying not to laugh aloud.

Georgette called to Katherine. "You're the matriarch, Katherine. Kindness is for chumps when you have a demon in your midst."

Charles's shout of laughter didn't silence Georgette as he pulled her away.

"I am so tired of people using their families as their own personal—personal—" She wasn't quiet while she raged. Lucy, Janey, and Robert stared in shock but they all had growing smiles. "A family of orphans would understand. Isn't that true?"

"I suppose it takes being an orphan," Marian said quietly. "It takes losing to appreciate having a family."

Georgette didn't argue. None of the people with her would. Lucy, Janey, and Eddie had lost both parents within days of each other from an illness. Robert and Joseph—not that he was with them—had lost their parents in an auto accident. Georgette had lost her father while she was at school and her mother just after she'd left school at a mere eighteen years old. Charles's parents had died, he'd lost his brother, his sister-in-law, and had been left with boys to see through school and into their careers. A big thriving family like the Lynds? Turning on each other?

It would never happen to her family.

"You're supposed to treasure family," she said loudly,

hoping the Lynds would hear. "Take care of them. You're supposed to—damn it!"

"It's Sunday, Georgette," Charles said, still grinning. "You're going straight to hell now."

"Charles!" Marian hissed. "Georgette! Language!"

"The vicar heard you!" Lucy hissed. "And Dr. West."

"Are they laughing or crying?" Robert countered. "If they're not laughing, they aren't our sort of people."

"The doctor is laughing," Janey said. "He has nice eyes."

"He looks like a baby." Robert picked up Janey, setting her on his shoulder.

"Robert! I'm too big!"

"Never," he replied. "Not ever! I used to be the family baby. Now it is you, darling."

Once they were away from the Lynds, Georgette calmed down and then gasped. "What is wrong with me? I —I—I shouted at that woman. After church! With everyone looking on."

"And you were marvelous," Charles told her and kissed her with everyone looking on.

ROBERT AARON

"What do we do, Eunice?" Robert asked merrily. He took a seat at the kitchen table, Janey at his side. "Georgette is causing a ruckus in the streets. Joseph is refusing to worship." Robert laughed after that. "Though that might have been because of Charles and me. We did, after all, comfort him with whiskey and tobacco. I made him food, you know. Gave him aspirin, but I've noticed men who've fallen in love and become family types can't keep up with young bachelors like myself. Of course, that means I have no idea what we do now."

"What do you mean what do we do?" Eunice asked dryly. "I don't know."

"What do you mean you don't know?" Robert demanded. "Eunice, heart of my heart, if you don't know, how can the rest of us continue?"

"Get a book, curl up, read it," Eunice told him. "Sundays are for dinners, naps, and reading."

❧ 13 ❧

GEORGETTE DOROTHY AARON

"Joseph didn't come to dinner," Marian said in a hushed voice as night approached. "Or church. The trains aren't running, so he must be at our—the —cottage."

"I know," Georgette replied as quietly, lifting her brows. "What should we do about that?"

"I need to talk to him."

Georgette nodded.

"Will you walk with me? Maybe shove me a little if I start to cry?"

"Are you going to break him?"

Marian shook her head.

"Because he said I was the matriarch of this family."

Marian laughed a watery noise. "Is that why you shouted that at Katherine? To remind her that she was the matriarch?"

"Yes," Georgette agreed, taking a torch from the top of her closet and leading the way outside. "Of course. As the matriarch, I will have to do something. As I don't know how to be a matriarch, it will probably be the wrong thing."

Marian tucked her arm through Georgette's, laying her head against Georgette's shoulder as they started towards the back garden. Marian paused at the turn to Joseph's cottage and hesitated.

She nudged Georgette the other way. "I need to work it out in my head. I might sick up. I'm so nervous. I feel so bad. Why am I so stupid?"

"You aren't."

"I—"

"When I was marrying Charles," Georgette cut in, letting Marian tug her down the path and through the woods. Dusk had come and gone and it was late to be wandering the wood, but they were together and they had come to know this portion of the wood well. "I was a pendulum of peace and needing to sick up myself. It was terrifying even well past the wedding date. I think I didn't truly calm down and stay calm until a couple of weeks past our wedding. I even made Charles give me space on our honeymoon because being around him all the time was suffocating me."

"Really?" Marian asked, sounding as though she'd seen an unexpected light in the darkness.

"Really," Georgette said. "Charles keeps track of whether I have enough space and makes sure I get it. It's why Janey is at school. She was spending so much time next to me, and I was starting to suffocate again. That, and of course, we'd send our own child to school."

"I didn't realize—"

Before Marian could finish, they realized that there was shouting at the Lynd house.

"I wouldn't have thought Katherine's family was so volatile," Georgette whispered, tucking the torch behind her back. "She's so calm."

The lights were on in the house, shining onto the lawn where the three Lynd brothers were shouting at each other. Georgette was shocked to see that John was shouting as much as his younger brothers.

Katherine came out and saw Georgette and Marian. She hissed something to her sons. All three of them fell silent and then disappeared. Katherine crossed to Georgette and Marian as though each step were painful. Georgette rushed forward when Katherine stumbled.

Georgette grabbed Katherine and wrapped an arm around her shoulders. Her older friend was trembling.

"I'm sorry," Georgette said. "We were avoiding our own troubles. We didn't mean to intrude on yours."

Katherine started to speak, shook her head, tried again, and then finally croaked out, "I need you to get Detective Aaron. There's been a terrible accident."

Georgette felt the hair on the back of her neck rise. "What happened?"

"Lizette is dead," Katherine cried. "She's dead. Oh my heavens, Georgette, she's dead."

Georgette's stomach dropped, and her eyes closed with dismay.

"You need Joseph," Marian said precisely. "Georgette, give me the torch. I'll go."

Georgette shook her head. There was no way they were separating when someone had died. Georgette grabbed Marian's wrist tightly and directed the torch at the path. Katherine didn't have a telephone, so the nearest point of contact was either Joseph's snug cottage or Georgette's home or to the Mustly's once again. Marian started and Georgette pushed herself to keep up. Marian was certainly more spry, but neither of them were willing to let the other go.

It took too long, what felt like forever, to reach Joseph's cottage. They darted towards the door, ignoring their surroundings in their hurry.

"What are you doing here?"

Marian screamed and Georgette would have but for being out of breath. They both turned to the corner of the little porch and realized that Joseph and Robert were sitting on rocking chairs, smoking in the dark.

"Are you all right?" Robert asked, moving quickly towards them. Georgette shook her head, still gasping while Marian ignored Joseph's anger to throw herself in his arms.

"Lizette Lynd is dead."

Both of the brothers cursed, and Joseph snapped, "Robert, take them to Charles, send for the doctor and the constable." Robert nodded and then Joseph cursed again. "No, put them in the auto. It'll take a moment to drop you at the house while I circle round to Katherine's home."

The car was silent for the few minutes drive. It wasn't all that much quicker than walking through the wood, but Georgette was still a bit winded. She laughed, still out of air, so it was more of a huffing croak.

"Your—your faces." She laughed into Marian's

shoulder and then realized that she'd started to cry. "Oh g-g-goodness."

Marian wrapped Georgette tightly and whispered to the alarmed Joseph and Robert, "It's just the baby."

If anything, their alarm escalated.

"No! No! The baby is fine, it just makes her emotions run the full gamut of possibility. Georgette loves Katherine."

Georgette nodded, wiping away a tear and fighting for her voice. "She's so sad. She was trembling. Her sons were fighting. It was awful. It was so, so awful. I want Charles."

They had reached her house and Joseph laid on the horn while nudging Robert and Marian from the auto. "I have to rush. Robert, make the calls."

Robert nodded and tugged Georgette towards the house, but Charles came rushing out. He was followed by Eunice in her nightdress and robe, and Lucy.

"Are you all right?" Charles asked.

"Just winded," Georgette admitted. "I'm fine."

"Lizette Lynd is dead," Robert told Charles, who cursed. "We need the doctor and the constables."

"I can do that," Lucy said immediately, her gaze lingering on Georgette and Marian before she spun and ran inside.

Georgette let Charles lead her inside because he seemed to calm when his hands were on her and he could feel that she was all right.

"What was it?" Charles asked. He wasn't asking if it was murder, but they were all wondering. Had Lizette had a complication from her wound? Had she done something to herself. Had someone ended her life? Georgette couldn't answer.

They made their way to the parlor and Eunice came in with tea, but she didn't leave. It was late, but they all wanted to know. They heard an auto go by and then another. The quickest route to Katherine's house was by Georgette and Charles's home. A few minutes later, Barnaby and Anna knocked on the door and Charles brought them in. They'd obviously dressed hastily.

In the silence of the parlor, they drank their tea and worried. It was oppressive until Barnaby said, "It must be murder."

"Or complications from the injury," his wife added, frowning deeply.

Georgette refilled her tea as Robert said, "I think that would make it murder still."

"I wonder if they'll refuse to talk," Lucy said and then blushed deeply when everyone looked at her. Her voice had fallen in volume, but she added, "If Eddie or Janey had killed someone—especially someone I didn't like—I might not help them be found."

Georgette's brows rose and Lucy flushed even more deeply, turning a shocking red. Robert, however, nodded. "I understand. Joseph or Charles kills some blight on humanity and I'm not going to help the constables. They're family."

Georgette rubbed the back of her neck. She was both morally opposed to everything they were saying and also entirely in agreement. If Charles—not that he would—murdered someone, would she turn him in? A part of her liked to think that her morals would rule, but Georgette wasn't sure that they would. Choose between Charles or anyone else? She would choose Charles every time.

"We might all be monsters," Georgette muttered. "I'm not sure I'd behave any differently. Sorry Barnaby and Anna, I would probably let you get caught."

"Same," Barnaby said with a laugh, letting Charles fill the bourbon Barnaby had taken over the tea.

"But anyone else in here? I don't know. I just don't know."

"We've become calloused," Charles said. "We've seen too much terrible."

Barnaby frowned. "What happened with Dr. Fowler was bad, but I think you can hang on."

The rest of them, except Lucy, paused. If only it were just Dr. Fowler, Georgette thought. She laughed without amusement and then took a deep sip of her tea.

"You know what we need?" Eunice asked. "Cake."

Robert shifted.

"It's unfortunate that the one I slaved over yesterday disappeared."

"Eunice," Robert said, trying a charming grin. "Who would do such a thing?" Like Eunice, he answered his own question. "A monster. But, I believe I saw some biscuits in the pantry. I'll get them, shall I?"

He rose and hurried from the room.

"I have cake," Anna said.

Barnaby laughed as he told his wife, "They're changing the subject on us."

"Yes," she said, "I know, darling. But my stomach is sour thinking of Katherine, so maybe a sweet will make things easier for our friends."

Georgette preferred her sweets when she was happy. When she was upset, she wanted nothing but tea. She rose and crossed to the window. It was late. "I don't think we're going to find out anything this evening. Night really."

The grandfather clock in the library rang to accent Georgette's comments, and it seemed that each of them counted each chime of the clock. When it stopped after a single dong, Georgette had little doubt each of them had to agree. There was no way that Joseph would return and answer their questions.

As a group, they started rustling and rising. Barnaby held out his arm to Anna, and she took it and then kissed Georgette on the cheek. "I'll be checking on Katherine tomorrow."

Georgette nodded, glancing at Charles. She could already guess that he wasn't going to be working in London tomorrow. Lucy and Eunice faded down the hall along with Marian while Charles and Georgette saw Anna and Barnaby to the door. Just as it shut, Robert appeared with a tin of butter biscuits.

"Have they gone?" Robert asked.

Charles nodded while Georgette sighed.

"This is horrible," she told them both. "I'm going to try to pretend it didn't happen."

"Do you need the biscuits?" Robert already had the tin open, and he grinned before popping one into his mouth. "I'm a callous soul who's glad this Lynd woman isn't one of the people I care about. I believe I'll sleep like a baby."

"Babies wake often, crying, in their own mess," Georgette said as she took a biscuit. Thinking of babies made her think of her own little Frederick or Anna. The case would be over before the baby arrived and better days were ahead.

Charles laughed at Robert's expression as Georgette turned towards the bedroom and then said dryly, "You're going to get several stones if you carry on as you are."

❧ 14 ☙

JOSEPH AARON

Joseph would like to say that he was focused on the job, but he knew it was a lie. He was focused on what it meant that Marian threw herself into his arms the previous night. Was she simply afraid, and he had been a protector for her at one time? Did it mean more? Was Georgette's theory that he didn't have the full information correct?

He didn't know. He took the auto back to the Lynd house. Lizette had been taken away late the previous night after Dr. West said that she'd 'certainly' been smothered. Joseph had nodded and then ordered the constables to send her body to one of the Yard doctors. Dr. West might be entirely right. Joseph's instincts had agreed. But the man looked like a pimply-faced schoolboy and Joseph wanted the support of someone who was an accepted professional. Even if Dr. West was the most learned doctor in England, it was hard to take the poor man seriously.

Joseph slowly got out of his auto and faced the house. He approached as the duo of Lynd brothers once again stepped outside. "Now's not a good time, Detective. We're a family in mourning."

Jedediah didn't say a word, but his expression was intractable.

"You're a family harboring a murderer," Joseph replied flatly. "The options of not answering questions is past."

The brothers were entirely unbothered. Was Joseph going to have to pull the entire family into Scotland Yard and question them ruthlessly?

"You're digging yourselves a hole here," Joseph snapped. "The next time I come back, you won't like the result if you continue to block the investigation. This is a murder, and it's not going to stand."

Mitchell lifted a brow and Jedediah cursed and walked back into the house. Joseph wondered just what it would take for them to answer questions? A member of this house had murdered another member and the result was that they were avoiding questions to protect a killer.

Joseph returned to the police station, waiting for the constables to come in. He thought it would work better to bring in the family members one-by-one. Why let them stand together? Joseph rubbed the back of his neck and dug through the desk until he found a bottle of aspirin.

"Higgins," Joseph said as the man entered. "Go get John Lynd. Don't take no for an answer."

Higgins's eyes widened and he nodded.

"We're done being nice," Joseph continued. "Bring him in shackled if necessary."

Joseph waited until John Lynd arrived and then took him to an uncomfortable chair and sat across from the fellow. He had dark circles under his eyes; the white of the eyes were bloodshot. The man shifted uncomfortably and coughed. Joseph leaned back, crossing his arms over his chest and stared, deliberately waiting long minutes.

John Lynd didn't seem to notice the passing of time. He stared at the wall, silent and seemingly lost.

"Who hurt your wife?"

John blinked rapidly as if surprised by the question that had finally come. His voice was a croak when he answered, "I don't know."

"Why was she here last Thursday?"

"I don't know," John said again. His gaze had returned to the wall. "I don't know anything."

"Do you know that most women are murdered by their husbands, fathers, or brothers?"

John didn't answer. Joseph wasn't entirely sure that John was aware of what was going on.

"You do realize that your wife is dead."

John shook his head slightly and then propped his face into his hands. "I—I don't feel well." He gagged a little and then started heaving. Joseph cursed and thrust the waste bin at the man. He didn't actually sick up, but he gagged horribly until Joseph's stomach was roiling. When the man finally quieted, he was weeping into the bin and Joseph shook his head.

"Call Dr. West," he said to Higgins, "and take John to the cell bed. Go lie down man," he told John. "We'll get someone to help you."

Higgins cajoled John Lynd to the cell bed and then went for the doctor. When he returned, Joseph said, "Go get another Lynd. I don't care which one."

Jedediah Lynd was the next to arrive, and he took the uncomfortable seat on the other side of the desk. "When was Lizette found?" Joseph demanded.

Jedediah didn't answer right away, so Joseph added, "Georgette Aaron noticed the ruckus outside of your house around 9:00 p.m." He'd kept Marian out of it on purpose, unable to say her name at the moment.

"We hadn't been outside long," Jedediah said vaguely. "Not sure how long really. It was a bit of a mess. We'd realized she'd died in her sleep just before."

"She didn't die in her sleep," Joseph snapped. "She was murdered."

"I don't know anything about that," Jedediah said, firmly meeting Joseph's gaze. "I can't imagine someone would want to kill a country housewife."

"But someone did," Joseph taunted. "Someone in your house."

"I don't know anything about that," Jedidiah said.

"Why did your sister-in-law come to Harper's Hollow? She must have known Katherine wouldn't be at home."

"I don't know," Jedidiah said, shrugging.

From that point on, every question Joseph asked was answered with either 'I don't know' or 'I don't know anything about that.'

Joseph slammed from the small room a few minutes later and met Higgins's gaze. "They're stonewalling again."

The constable shrugged enough to tell Joseph that he wasn't surprised.

"Should we arrest them all?" Joseph demanded. "They're conspiring together to cover up a murder."

Higgins answered slowly. "I don't know. But—they can't all be on the same page. I don't think that Katherine Lynd would agree to what's happening here. Known her since I was in short pants, and I can't see it."

"So you're saying we should pressure the ladies?" Joseph snarled. "Go get Mitchell Lynd. Once we have Mitchell, send Jedediah out and then follow him. Don't be sneaky. Walk a few paces behind him and watch his every move. Have young Mattie watch their house. Again, stand in the open, watch the house, talk to the children, search the garden even though you know there's nothing there to find, ask questions every time someone steps outside. Ask questions of everyone who approaches the door. Be overt and obnoxious."

Neither of them was pleased with the plan, but as long as the family refused to talk, what could they do? Joseph ran over the family members in his head. John Lynd, the husband. Mitchell Lynd, the defacto oldest, given John's injury and passive personality. Jedediah Lynd, the farmer. Katherine Lynd. Emmanuline Lynd. The two wives, Margaret and Jane. Only the son, Brent, wasn't involved, living too far away.

On the day of Lizette being attacked only Katherine and Mitchell had a reliable witness to speak to their location. On the day of the murder, the family had been together. They had known who attacked Lizette, but she'd been acting odd. It wasn't necessarily true that whoever attacked her with the fence post had been the person to murder her.

Joseph cursed and then cursed again and called Higgins back. "Get Margaret Lynd instead."

The constable nodded, brows lifted and left the police station.

Joseph waited until the constable had been gone long enough to reach the Lynd house before telling Jedediah to leave. He gave the man a fierce scolding, but the man only nodded before walking causally away.

The moment he was gone, Joseph smiled evilly. Margaret Lynd was Jedediah's wife, and he was going to be furious when he realized they'd timed things for Jedediah not to realize Margaret was being questioned until it was too late.

She arrived a quarter hour after her husband had left and she came in white-faced and alarmed. Her cheeks were flushed with rings of red, and her eyes showed signs of having cried. Joseph left her sitting long enough to bring the doctor from the cell to just outside the office.

"Mrs. Lynd," Joseph snapped, making himself sound harsh. "Your husband is suspected of murder."

"He wouldn't have," she said tremulously. "He's a good Christian man. This is all a terrible accident."

"It's murder."

Margaret Lynd didn't answer.

"Who killed Lizette?" His voice was gentle that time and Margaret looked up with swimming eyes.

"I don't know."

For the first time, Joseph actually believed a Lynd. "Do you know who hurt her the other day?"

Margaret shook her head quickly, but he thought he'd found her lie. Was she lying to protect her husband?

Husband or someone else? "It must not be murder. How could it be?"

Joseph wasn't nearly as kind when he answered. "Someone took a pillow and held it over Lizette Lynd's face until she died. She died, lungs burning, terrified, murdered by someone she thought of as family."

Margaret gasped and the tears started. Dr. West stepped into the room then and Joseph silently applauded the doctor's sense of timing.

Slowly Margaret looked up to the doctor and asked, "Is that true?"

"It is."

If only the poor man didn't look quite so much like a schoolboy. Joseph saw the doubt seep into Margaret Lynd's gaze as she examined the doctor.

"It's being confirmed by Scotland Yard," Joseph told her flatly. "But there's little doubt. Just think—your children are in that house. They're in the same house with a killer. Will they be next?"

It was the wrong tack. Her eyes blazed with fury as she hissed, "I don't know who killed Lizette. I was sitting with the children reading to them when Katherine started screaming, but I can tell you this. She was a monster, and I'm not sorry she's gone."

Joseph frowned as Margaret Lynd rose. "We're not done here."

"I won't speak to you further without my husband. Arrest me or get him. The only reason I came was because he was supposed to be here."

Joseph let her go.

"Why doesn't anyone believe me when I say she was murdered?" Dr. West asked with frustration.

"Because you look like you're playing doctor after having stolen your instruments from a real doctor."

Dr. West flushed.

"It'll get better in time, man," Joseph said almost kindly. "You've a hard road here, looking as you do."

He scowled as he replied, "I think you should let John Lynd go. I suspect he has a heart condition on top of everything else. He needs medicine and care or he'll be dead in a year."

Joseph gestured at the door and said, "Might as well. Those brothers decided in advance on their course of action. We need a crowbar to make them talk, but I don't know what that is. Not yet."

15

GEORGETE DOROTHY AARON

Georgette crossed to visit Anna the next morning and found both Anna and Katherine in the back garden.

"Oh," Georgette said. "I'm—I didn't mean to intrude. Are you all right, Katherine?"

Katherine shook her head, pressing her handkerchief to her face. "I should have stayed home, but I couldn't breathe there."

Georgette sat down and took Katherine's free hand. There hadn't been an invitation, but Georgette ignored that niggling voice in her mind.

"What has been happening?" She kept her voice fused with sympathy and love, and Katherine pressed her handkerchief harder into her face.

Both Anna and Georgette waited as Katherine wept and struggled. Finally she said, "I'm not sure really."

"Do you know who injured Lizette last week?"

Katherine shook her head. "My children realized which of them did it and they banded together. They wouldn't tell me. Even Emmanuline knows, but she won't say a word."

Georgette looked towards her own garden. What if their wards had done the same? Georgette immediately realized that it would be Janey who was the criminal of the three. Eddy was too focused on his goals. Lucy was too kind and responsible. Janey was the one who was full of mischief. Without other factors, Georgette could guess in her family, and they'd only had the orphans for a few short months.

She nibbled on her thumb as she considered further. What would a woman like Katherine guess? She knew her children well, she probably knew why Lizette had come to her house, she could guess how each of them might react.

"You know who hurt Lizette though, don't you? Even without a confession, you have a good idea."

"I don't know anything," Katherine replied, "and I don't necessarily think that the person who...who..."

"Who hit Lizette with a fence post," Georgette filled in. The worse were harsh, but her tone was gentle.

Katherine nodded, wiped her face again, and then said, "That one. I don't...I don't...I don't think that they were the one who...who...who..."

Georgette was a little less patient when she filled in, "Who smothered your daughter-in-law?"

Katherine flinched.

Anna finally spoke. "You know that one of your children was the one who injured Lizette. And either that same child or another one murdered her."

Katherine's tears were falling as she nodded. "I have a guess as to who might have injured Lizette."

"Who?" Georgette demanded.

Katherine shook her head. "I know my children well. I know who might snap in anger, but—I would have sworn to you without hesitation that none of them would have hurt Lizette or anyone else."

"Hurt?" Anna used the same unequivocal but gentle tone that Georgette had. "They killed Lizette, Katherine. Why did Lizette come here?"

It took Katherine a while to gather herself, and Georgette was shocked when her friend answered. "Lizette had been cooking up a plan."

Neither Georgette nor Anna dared to breathe or ask a question.

"She wanted to sell my property, have me move in with Emmanuline, and split the money from the sale. She had been hinting at it. That it was only right. That they were suffering. That John was hurt and needed help."

Georgette's shock bled away. It was new information to either of them. She and Anna had discussed it before, but Katherine didn't seem to realize it.

"She thought I should give them everything I have."

"But Gregory is buried in your orchard," Anna said.

"I know," Katherine said, closing her eyes. "Lizette said he was gone and the location of his body no more mattered than me clinging to the remnants of a life that just hadn't petered out yet."

"My heavens," Anna muttered. Her tone made it clear that she would have been tempted to knock Lizette Lynd down with a fencepost herself.

"That's why she spoke about avarice on Sunday,"

Georgette said. "You were clinging to your riches by refusing to give them to her."

Katherine nodded. "It got worse. When we returned from church, Lizette made it clear that I could sell my property or she'd tell who hurt her."

"She intended to blackmail you into giving up everything you own?"

Katherine nodded, still crying.

"What did your sons have to say?"

"They dared her to do it. Jed and Mitch did anyway. I'm not sure John even realized what she was saying. He's always loved her. It's like the moment he decided he loved her, he could never see another flaw."

"That's a pretty big flaw to miss," Georgette said without sympathy.

"He's a dreamer," Katherine said. "He doesn't live in the same world as the rest of us. Do you know why he was injured? He was daydreaming and forgot one of the steps for safety. While he recovered, he wrote the same story that distracted him in a series of short stories." Katherine shook her head, baffled. "They were terrible, but he pinned all his hopes on getting them published. He's been sending them to publishing house after publishing house. He even thought of approaching your Charles, Georgette, but it seems that Charles already turned him down."

Georgette winced and then flinched further when Katherine added, "Twice."

"I—"

"Don't apologize," Katherine told Georgette. "Charles isn't running a charity and John's stories really are bad."

"Has anyone heard from Joseph?" Georgette asked when she returned home. Katherine wouldn't speak any more on the subject of Lizette, so Georgette left the two friends together.

Charles nodded. "He stopped in to use our telephone to call his supervisor. He didn't want to be overheard. Did you learn something?"

Georgette recapped her conversation and then said, "I have an idea, but—"

"But you feel bad about it after hearing what Lizette was up to?" Charles suggested. "I'll call the police office and see if we can get Joseph here. You can tell him your plan."

Georgette nodded. She paced the parlor until Joseph arrived along with Dr. West and one of the constables. Marian had been watching from the corner and the way the two met each other's gaze was painful to see. Before Georgette could begin, Eunice came into the parlor.

"There's a telephone call for you, Marian. It's your mother."

Marian closed her eyes and nodded, excusing herself. The look on her face was fierce as she approached the library where the phone was housed.

"Georgette?" Joseph demanded. His tone told her that he wasn't waiting for Marian. Fierce and hurt.

Georgette sighed and then began. "I think I might know who injured Lizette. Katherine knows who it was and she's not convinced it is the same person who killed Lizette. In fact, I would guess that Katherine is positive that they aren't the same person."

"Who do you think struck down Lizette?"

Before answering, Georgette explained what had been

happening in the Lynd family. When she reached the end of the tale, Joseph cursed, a nasty habit he was forming, in Georgette's opinion, and Dr. West swallowed thickly.

"That's not right," Dr. West said. "Lizette Lynd's plan is not right."

"You won't get an argument from Georgette," Charles told him. "She would be an avenging angel if not that the engineer of such madness weren't already dead."

Georgette murmured a hushed agreement and then added, "I would bet the proceeds of my next book that Katherine offered John and Lizette a place in her home. Combining households would have eased everyone's burden, but I am also betting Lizette refused."

"Who do you think struck Lizette down?"

"Emmanuline," Georgette said. "Notice that her husband and children aren't here. I asked Anna about it, and she said Emmanuline's in-laws watch the children whenever she wants. Katherine was providing service, the brothers all have work, the other Lynd women have children as well, but may not have ready caretakers to leave them."

Joseph paused. "It's all guesses."

"But they make sense," Charles added. "They make a lot of sense, really. Emmanuline is probably the one who looks after Katherine the most. Mothers can have a strong influence over their daughters."

Joseph shot Charles a black look.

"They do," Georgette agreed. "Daughters are also the ones who become the confidant of a mother's worries. How many times did Katherine tell Emmanuline that she felt closer to her deceased husband in her own house?"

"What is your plan?" Joseph asked Georgette.

"Wait a moment," Dr. West cut in. "I think there's more to be said here."

"Oh?" Joseph asked.

"It actually makes a fair amount of sense that it was Emmanuline who injured Lizette because Lizette didn't die."

"And?" Joseph's expression said to get to the point.

"Lizette was a strong woman," Dr. West said. "I noticed that when tending to her. She was also much larger than Emmanuline who is, I believe, a mother not a farmer's wife?"

Georgette nodded in answer to Dr. West's question.

"I don't think Emmanuline would be strong enough to smother Lizette Lynd. It's been on my mind all day, actually. The woman would not have suffocated without struggling. I think holding her down would have been possible only by one of the brothers."

"You didn't think to tell me this before?" Joseph snapped.

"It's been on my mind." Dr. West shrugged. "I wanted to consider. Jedediah Lynd is most likely the stronger, but John Lynd could have used his bulk."

"What about Mitchell Lynd?" Joseph asked, obviously taking to the idea. "He's my bet. Family leader, mother threatened. He didn't love Lizette. He's taken charge this whole time."

"I think," Georgette said, "you might easily get a confession."

"How?" Joseph demanded.

"You need to drive a wedge between those brothers and make them turn on each other."

"Yes," Joseph growled. "I've been trying."

"But you aren't using the right force. You have to arrest someone who they love more than they love each other. Someone they want to protect. Someone they've been protecting."

"Georgette," Charles breathed, staring at her in shock. "Do you mean Emmanuline?"

She was dry-eyed as she nodded. Joseph shook his head. "I'll need to talk to my superior before I do such a mad thing, knowing she is probably not the killer."

Georgette felt sick at her idea, and she went to her room the moment Joseph left, taking the doctor with him. Marian came into Georgette's room and found her on the bed with dogs surrounding her. She climbed in next to Georgette.

"Mother demanded I return home. She was furious I didn't leave this morning and more furious when I told her what was happening."

Georgette closed her eyes. The headache that had been building since the previous night stabbed at her. It came and went with her morning sickness, but lingered whenever she was tired, upset, or assaulted by paint fumes.

"What did you say?"

"I told her no. She said she didn't know me anymore. That you and Joseph had turned me from a tractable daughter to a demon."

Georgette winced for Marian, hearing the pain in her friend's voice. She reached out her hand and clutched Marian's. She could smell the salt of tears, and all she could offer was a hand. It seemed to be enough. Marian cried quietly and somehow, they both slipped into sleep.

❧ 16 ❧

JOSEPH AARON

"Do you think it will work?" Higgins asked as Joseph motored to the Lynd house.

Joseph considered for a moment. "Georgette is usually right about people. Those brothers love Emmanuline. They might confess to having done it even if it was her."

"But it wasn't?"

"Probably not," Joseph said, hearing the distraction in his own voice. Certainly, Mrs. Parker had been calling Marian home. It might well be the last time he saw her as his betrothed and he had a murderer to catch. Her parents had a point about his work, he thought as he stopped his auto in front of the Lynd house.

Before he'd even taken two steps from the auto door, Mitchell Lynd appeared outside the house. His gaze was furious. "What now? Can't you see we're still mourning?"

"Additional information has come in," Joseph told Mitchell flatly. "Step aside."

"Additional information?"

Joseph didn't answer, instead bypassing the Lynd son. Was this the one who had murdered Lizette Lynd? Mitchell had Joseph's vote, but he suddenly wondered who Georgette suspected. He should have asked before he'd left the house, but he wasn't playing his best game with this case.

Joseph let himself into the house. The parlor contained all the Lynd siblings, Brent having arrived that day, their mother, as well as the vicar. Only the children and the wives of the brothers were missing. With Joseph, the constable, and the doctor, the house felt bursting at the seams.

"Detective?" Katherine asked shakily.

"I'm afraid I've come to arrest one of your children on suspicion of murder, Katherine." Joseph used his gentlest voice.

She gasped and leaned into her daughter, which made the next sentence all the more terrible.

"Emmanuline Smith, would you please come with me?"

She gasped.

"You were seen after your attack on Lizette Lynd."

"That doesn't mean she killed Lizette," Jedediah shouted. "She's gentle and kind."

"She struck down another woman and left her unconscious and abandoned," Joseph replied flatly. "Of course she's the killer."

"She's not," Katherine said, shaking her head and crying. "Not my Emmy. Not my Emmy. No. No no no no no no no." Katherine's sobbing had the vicar taking her hand while her children stared at each other in shock.

Slowly, Emmanuline stood and took a step towards Joseph, but Katherine grabbed her wrist as if to save her.

"You're wrong," Mitchell said hoarsely. "It wasn't Emmanuline."

"You and your family have stonewalled the investigation at every turn. I understand, Lynd, you were protecting your sister. But the game's up."

"Emmanuline?" Brent looked confused and then angry, so similar to Jedidiah that Joseph might have suspected him if he'd been anywhere near the area and without an alibi.

"You don't understand anything," Jedediah shouted. "You have no evidence."

"I have a woman who attacked another woman. I have a dead body. I have opportunity and a history of violence."

"It's all right," Emmanuline said quietly to Mitchell. "It's all right."

To Joseph's utter shock, a voice said, "No, it isn't."

Joseph slowly turned to look at the man who had finally spoken. "I killed Zette."

"No," Emmanuline said to her brother. "No, this is my fault."

"It's mine," John said, sounding exhausted. He unbuttoned the cuffs on his shirt as he spoke. "I should have heard what Zette was up to. I should have stopped it. It should have been me protecting Mum. Not you, Em."

"Are you saying you murdered your wife?" Joseph asked John Lynd.

In answer, he rolled up his cuffs and showed his scratched wrists. "I told her to leave Mother alone. I told her that Mother would live in her home until the day she died. I told her to stop. She laughed at me and called me a fool and said she didn't need me anymore. For the love of Emmanuline, the Lynd family would do anything."

His jaw was trembling and tears were flowing down his face.

"She was right. For the love of Emmanuline, the kindest of us, I would silence my own Zette."

Joseph nodded at Higgins who pulled John Lynd away. Joseph looked at the horrified family. "I'm sorry."

They weren't appeased but there was nothing else to say.

❧

"Was it John Lynd?" she asked when Joseph returned to her house.

He poured himself a large drink and lit a cigarette, taking a chair near the fire. "How did you know?"

"The other brothers would have lied for Emmanuline and each other, so Lizette's threat was meaningless. She was too self-absorbed to realize. So it seemed to me that only someone who hadn't been paying attention and had been living in a dreamland would snap hard enough to kill."

Charles lit his pipe, calm in the face of his wife's preternatural ability.

"You're a witch," Joseph said.

"And friends with a demon," his Marian answered from the doorway.

Joseph couldn't believe she was there, in the house. He

felt the first stirrings of hope. "Didn't your mother call you home?"

"She did," Marian replied. "I explained that she was ruining my life and my relationship with the man I love. I further added that she and Father had to understand that no matter how many cons they come up with regarding you, they'll never outweigh the pros that didn't even need to be written down."

"What pros are those?" Joseph asked, slowly rising to face her as the hope grew.

"That I don't want to live without you. That I love you. That you're my dream come true."

He stepped forward and took her face between his hands and kissed her soundly.

"Brava!" Georgette said. Joseph was barely aware of Charles lifting Georgette and carrying her from the parlor. "This is our house," Georgette laughed.

The last thing Joseph heard was the shout of Charles's laughter and the click of the parlor door. He let Marian go but she stepped closer to him.

"I thought I'd lost this," he told her.

"I love you, Joseph Aaron. Nothing will change that."

"What did Georgette call it?" he asked.

"Our happily ever after." She cupped his cheek and smiled up at him. "Will you build one with me?"

His answer was another fervent kiss.

❧

IF THERE WAS ONE THING THE GODDESS ATË LOVED, IT was a destruction caused by your own stupidity. Lizette Lynd had her downfall. What could be better? Her gaze turned to the village, seeing end after end approaching and she wondered just how they would go. Curiosity was the greatest gift to endless life, outside of surprise. Would Georgette surprise again? What about the far more prosaic Marian Parker? Young Lucy? That minx in progress, Janey? The possibilities were endless.

The END

Hullo friends! I am so grateful you dove in and read the latest Vi book. If you wouldn't mind, I would be so grateful for a review.

The sequel to this book is available now.

Christmas 1937

Georgette Dorothy Aaron has found her dream home, her dream village, and her dream husband. She and Charles are ready to dive into their holidays and create their own ideal traditions. When they're drawn into an unexpected mystery, they little expect what follows. Except for one thing, the reliable goodness of their friends and family.

Join Georgette and those she loves as they dive into the intrigue working around an excess of time next to the fire, milky tea, and Christmas treats.

Order your copy here.

My newest series is now available. Keep on flipping for a sneak peak.

April 1922

When the Ku Klux Klan appears at the door of the Wode sisters, they decide it's time to visit the ancestral home in England.

With squabbling between the sisters, it takes them too long to realize that their new friend is being haunted. Now they'll have to set aside their fight, discover just why their friend is being haunted, and what they're going to do about it. Will they rid their friend of the ghost and out themselves as witches? Or will they look away?

Join the Wodes as they rise up and embrace just who and what they are in this newest historical mystery adventure.

Order Your Copy Here or keep on scrolling for the first chapter.

SNEAK PEEK OF BRIGHT
YOUNG WITCHES & THE
RESTLESS DEAD

CHAPTER ONE

APRIL 1922. WASHINGTON D.C. USA

ARIADNE EUDORA WISTERIA WODE

"Give me some of the good stuff," the man said, nudging a
waiting girl aside. He was wearing a pinstriped evening
suit with his hair pomaded back. Given the large ring on
his pinky and the gold on his watch chain, Ariadne
assumed he was quite wealthy or quite powerful or both.
The large cigar hanging from his mouth suggested both.

Ariadne had been just behind him when he went
shoving people about and she caught the girl he'd sent
stumbling off her bar stool. The height of the girl's heels
didn't help, but the man hadn't even noticed he'd knocked
the woman down. The girl shot him a nasty, unnoticed
look and then turned to Ariadne with a glance that said,
Can you believe this dirty bloke?

"We're out," the barman said. "Want a Coke?"

The shelves behind him were nearly empty of bottles, unlike the bar itself, which was full. Ariadne sighed. The speakeasy never ordered enough, always ran low, and then the boss took it out on her. He needed either more suppliers, to quit under-ordering, or to open a little less often. Some of the fellows in the bar were reeling drunk and could have been cut off before they'd reached that state. Sloppy drunks put everyone at risk of getting pinched.

"Give me what the management is drinking," the man growled. "I know you got the good stuff, and I don't want any of this second-rate swill that'll leave me blind or dead."

"Our delivery of the good stuff is late," the barman said flatly. Whoever this shove-y man was, the barman was unimpressed. "No one's drinking much until that comes along. Not even the boss man."

Ariadne met the barman's gaze, and he jerked his head to the back. There was a triggerman guarding the door, and the man didn't move when Ariadne approached. His dark eyes fixed on hers, and there was threat in his stony expression.

Here we go again, Ariadne thought, ignoring his look and sliding past him without a flicker of a lash. Posturing was such a gent's move. She had too much to do for this nonsense. When she felt someone watching her, she glanced back and caught the gaze of a bloke with dark, sharp eyes and slicked back hair, with a hefty drink in front of him. He was, she thought, almost certainly a copper. Hopefully he was dirty. Otherwise, they'd all be hauled away with time in the slammer. The goons anyway. The shadows liked Ariadne.

Either way, she wished she was a little less memorable in the drop-waisted, shimmery dress that showed off far more of her chest than she'd prefer. She dressed with the intent to blend in with the other dames. Better to be seen as an easy moll than what she was—a lady-legger. Or, more accurately, a booze-making witch.

"It's about time," Blind Bobby growled as Ariadne appeared. "Do you have it? I don't pay full price for late goods. You're costing me a pile of lettuce, girl."

"They had checkpoints on the way in. I had to think quick and step even more quickly. You're lucky I'm here at all, and you'll be paying me the full amount or I'll take a walk down to the next juice joint. Easy peasy." She snapped her fingers. It was always better not to be too challenging, but sometimes she couldn't help herself.

Blind Bobby put his gun on the table and leaned back. "Maybe I'll just take the booze and pay you nothing, little girl."

"Did you find someone else who makes gin that won't blind you and can age wine and whisky with magic— because I don't think you have found anyone like me."

"I'll pay you eighty percent." He sniffed and growled, "From here on."

His dark, beady eyes fixed on her, and he leaned in, strong jaw gritted. He intended to scare her, but Ariadne was only irritated. She felt as though every time she interacted with this grunting beast, he thought he could just tower over her face and she'd crumple. Ariadne laughed, a trilling thing that didn't sound amused but conveyed her message.

Blind Bobby nudged his gun once again, and Ariadne scowled at him, dropping all pretense of amusement. She crossed her arms over her chest and lifted a challenging brow instead. "Do you really want to put a *bean* shooter up against magic?"

"Do you really want to put you and your little sister against my boys? There's even smaller witch brats in that town of yours. What's it called? Nighton? Bring her in." The last was said to one of the apes standing about grasping their guns trying to look intimidating.

There was a sound at the tunnel door and several men poured through with Ariadne's sister, Echo. She struggled in the grasp of...Ariadne's head cocked and gaze narrowed.

Lindsey Noel. She scowled at him. He was the shining son of Nighton and the fellow intent on finding his way into Ariadne's sister Circe's knickers.

"Well, if it isn't Lindsey Noel. Are you joining in on threatening my sisters? *All* of my sisters?"

Lindsey blushed, but his voice was mean. "I know where you live." His fingers dug into Echo's bicep.

"And I know where you live." Ariadne glanced at Echo, who seemed fine despite the white circles under Lindsey's pressing fingers. "Why'd you let them take you?"

"I wanted to see what Lindsey was up to. Sooner or later, Circe will see he's milquetoast playing at being a leading man. She believes that front he puts up, but the mannered handsome puppy will fade into what he really is —another arrogant rube with a rich daddy. It'll go easier if it's me telling her what he did, and after all—he put his hands on me."

Easier, Ariadne translated, than if Ari were the one

who told Circe her lover put them all at risk with his playing at being a bad boy.

The idiot Lindsey let go of Echo, but it was too late. The smirk she shot him was enough to have him wondering, would he lose Circe over this? The unfortunate answer was that Ariadne could only wish.

The other men glanced at each other, smirking, when Blind Bobby grunted, "No one cares about your hick problems." He gestured and the goons lining the wall leveled their guns at Ariadne.

She sighed. "Until I get paid, you won't be able to open the bottles at the delivery point. Try as you might."

Blind Bobby laughed meanly and Ariadne yawned. He shoved the table back, grabbing his gun as he did, and shoved it into Ariadne's face, pressing it hard against her forehead.

"Careful," she said quietly, "guns do malfunction so easily."

"Open the whiskey, Petey," Blind Bobby ordered.

Ariadne rolled her eyes and telepathically told her sister, *Draw your magic.* Ariadne opened her mind and senses to her own magic. She'd originally approached Blind Bobby once prohibition went into effect because the church basement where the speakeasy was housed was a place of power. Her magic, always strong, thrummed through her with a vengeance here. Echo's must be a tsunami of power given the dead that even Ariadne could sense.

The ghosts are restless, Echo sent.

Of course they are, it's a desecrated church. How did Noel know about us?

Echo's mental snort seemed to ricochet about

Ariadne's head and they both knew the answer: Circe. Soft, trusting, blind-with-love Circe. Lindsey Noel wasn't surprised in the least by their magic. Their sister hated keeping what they were from her 'sweet' Lindsey. She must have talked, and he'd gathered a full confession, given his presence.

Foolish girl.

The grunting of his man trying to open the bottle caught her attention. The goon was yanking at the stopper in the whiskey bottle, desperate to open it. He finally brought out a large knife, but it bounded off of the glass as though it were stone instead of a little bit of cork and glass. Finally he looked up at Blind Bobby and shook his head.

Blind Bobby pulled the gun back enough just to shove it back against her head again. "That's gonna leave a bruise." His laugh was ugly and he glanced at his men until they were snorting with unbelievable laughter as well.

"Balm of Gilead is an easy enough potion to make for someone like me," Ariadne told him, drawing her magic so deeply that her bobbed hair was slowly starting to rise around her face. "The bruise will be gone in minutes. I carry it in my handbag."

"What about the hole my bullet leaves?" He cocked his gun and then, to her horror, swung his arm wide, aiming at Echo. "Will it cure that?"

"Fool," Ariadne said, finished with this nonsense. She dropped to her knees, covering her head when the gun misfired, and magic rushed into Ariadne as the place of power energized her and she sent the rest of the guns into either misfiring or not firing at all.

With Echo there, ghosts were caught in the energy in the church and within the sisters. The ghosts went mad, merging into a tornado of shadows that sent Blind Bobby's goons into shrieking like little girls. Point of fact, Ariadne thought as she started to crawl away from Blind Bobby, her little sisters wouldn't have whined like these boys.

A moment later, the copper from earlier rushed the door. Ariadne dropped her magic immediately so it seemed that the screaming goons had gone crazy. On her knees, with forced tears, she looked like a victim as she reached for the copper. She screamed to draw his attention to her from Echo. "Help! Help me, please!"

Police swarmed the room, and Ariadne was yanked to her feet by the first copper to reach her. He glanced her over, muttered, "Fool doll," and shoved her behind him.

She shivered and whimpered and thanked the whole of the group repetitively with big crocodile tears, backing towards the wall. Her dress, her mussed makeup, and her tears were enough for the blokes to not realize she was one of the criminals. Just another doll caught up with the wrong man. She waited until they were all looking the other way, wrestling the goons down, and she slid into the shadows, pulling them around her.

The coppers didn't know about the escape tunnel where Echo had already disappeared, followed by Lindsey Noel. Echo had sealed it against any but Ariadne, so the fuzz were gathering up the men who couldn't use their tunnel while she slipped through, cloaked in darkness and magic.

Using the athamé in her handbag, Ariadne carved a rune of the door to keep it locked. She ignored the skittering of rats and the cool touch of the dead as she hurried down the tunnel.

"Go back to sleep," she murmured to the dead, hoping they'd comply. Otherwise the boys who worked for Blind Bobby would find themselves chilled in body and spirit.

The old church had a crypt underneath, so it was better not to look into the dark entrances of side rooms if you wanted to avoid looking at the remnants of the living. The tunnels went from the crypt to beyond the graveyard behind the church, following beneath the road. Blind Bobby's men had extended the tunnels even farther. With that kind of work ethic, what might those goons have been capable of if they bothered working for good?

Ariadne mocked herself—knowing she was a criminal too—and moved quickly through the tunnels. There were exits for a good mile down the tunnel road if you knew where to look and what to look for.

The vast majority of Ariadne's booze delivery was still in the auto garage where one of the exits from the tunnels led. The bottles were loaded on the back of her truck. Echo already had their truck running and was just loading the last of the whiskey bottles that had been previously unloaded. Any speakeasy could make gin in their bathtub. Magically aged liqueurs, wines, and whiskey required a witch, a different country, or a very expensive operation that risked prison time. Ariadne sealed the tunnel behind her with the same rune she'd used before. Someone would have to find the runes she'd used and destroy them before the exit would open. Otherwise it would take hours for the spell to fade.

She looked away from her spell and eyed her sister.

Echo looked a little mussed but none the worse for wear. "Anyone left here?"

"Just Timmy," Echo grunted as she grabbed the bag of their clothes from behind the truck's seat. "Poor boy. My spell got him hard in the gut when he tried to dodge. He'll have sore ribs if Blind Bobby doesn't kill him for losing us and the booze."

"Did Lindsey get out?" Ariadne asked as she shimmied out of her evening gown. Echo tossed Ariadne a wool skirt and blouse, and they stripped down in the auto garage, changing from party clothes to one step away from an initiate for a nunnery.

"He got out when I did, but he was bright enough not to follow me here. We need to consider a change of employment. If things had gone differently, Circe would be raising Medea and Cassiopeia. I love Circe, but..."

Ariadne winced. It was true. If there had been more coppers or if the fellows were a little more trigger happy, they'd have been in trouble. With enough guns blazing, even witches wouldn't have survived.

Ariadne told Echo, "Aunt Beatrix said she was interested in taking over. She has more people. That...that... flimflam that just happened to us wouldn't have happened to her. Not with her sons. Jasper and Gerard with those broad shoulders and thick jaws? Let alone their magic? They won't get the same garbage we're getting."

"We'll still get our cut too," Echo reminded Ariadne with a telling glance. "Beatrix promised it when she wanted to take on the work. You engineered the spells for aging the booze like we do, and Beatrix knows it. We have to be careful, Ariadne—at least until Medea and Cassiopeia are older. They're too little to lose you too."

It wasn't Echo's words that convinced Ariadne. It was the memory of the gun being swung her sister's way. If Echo hadn't been prepared for someone to turn their gun on her, if her magic hadn't been inclined towards the dead, if they'd been firing guns haphazardly, if the sisters had been a little less lucky, Ariadne might have lost her sister. No amount of dough was worth that.

Order Your Copy Here.

Christmas Madness: A Short Story Anthology

Hijinks & Murder

Love & Murder

A Zestful Little Murder (coming soon)

A Murder Most Odd (coming soon)

Nearly A Murder (coming soon)

THE POISON INK MYSTERIES

Death By the Book

Death Witnessed

Death by Blackmail

Death Misconstrued

Deathly Ever After

Death in the Mirror

A Merry Little Death

Death Between the Pages

THE 2ND CHANCE DINER MYSTERIES

(This series is complete.)

Spaghetti, Meatballs, & Murder

Cookies & Catastrophe

Poison & Pie

Double Mocha Murder

Cinnamon Rolls & Cyanide

Tea & Temptation

Donuts & Danger

Scones & Scandal

Lemonade & Loathing

Wedding Cake & Woe

Honeymoons & Honeydew

The Pumpkin Problem

THE HETTIE & RO ADVENTURES

cowritten with Bettie Jane

(This series is complete.)

Philanderer Gone

Adventurer Gone

Holiday Gone

Aeronaut Gone